THE FACTS & LEGENDS OF CALLIE CATWELL

THE FACTS & LEGENDS OF CALLIE CATWELL

SOPHIA DERISE

ZENITH PUBLISHING

For Ellie.
You're the sweetest person I know and the coolest sister of them all. Love you so, so much!

I SEE A LAKE MONSTER

AT LAKE VIEW Mobile Homes Park, we're having a misty morning. The sun hasn't burned the fog off of Lost Lake yet, and everything outside is quiet and still. The clouds are all caught up in the trees that rise above our little valley, and the sky is the kind of hazy yellow that promises a sunny day. Outside, it's my favorite kind of morning, which is great because right now, inside is sort of freaking me out.

Inside is where my dad is. And I love my dad. I really do. Which is why I can't be around him right now. Because right now is when we need to eat breakfast, and eating, for the past several years, makes him super uncomfortable.

He asked me to leave. I'm wondering if maybe I shouldn't have.

Lake View sits against the scuzzy end of a lake—Lost Lake—and there are ratty little rowboats and kayaks lined up in the tall grass along the water's edge. I don't think any of them belong to the people that live here. This isn't really the "I've got money to spare on a boat" kind of crowd. We're like the storage unit for the people with three-story houses a few miles up the bank: tucked away, hardly maintained.

I'm standing on the cement slab launch point that angles into the water. It's only a bit cold outside, which means that it's particularly warm for April. I've got my mom's old, scratchy blanket wrapped around me as I stand at the water's edge, just watching the mist come off the lake. It's all happening slowly—the rising sun, the evaporation. The day is starting right in front of me, but if I focus on any of it, it's impossible to see.

My phone buzzes, and I'm hoping it's Dad, but Rafael's name lights up my screen.

Don't stand me up Callie Cat!!!

At the end of his message there are at least nine little emojis because Raf doesn't know how to text like someone his age. He might as well be forty when he texts. Forty or four. Not sixteen, like he's supposed to be.

Most mornings, I meet Rafael at the gas station where he works at the top of the hill. If I time it right, he gets me free gas station coffee as he's leaving. And even though his shift usually ends at six a.m. (six a.m.!), I normally make it in time. But today, I don't think I will. I'm too worried to walk up a hill right now.

I debate going back inside. Dad's been doing better. I mean, better than before. There are still days like today, just not as many as there used to be, which is progress. I've gotta remember all this damn progress.

Another buzz. Not my dad. But it's Mei.

Tonight is the niiight playahhh!!!!

I laugh because I can hear her saying it. And because it's Mei. She always makes me laugh. She always makes things a little better.

She sends a follow up text before I can respond.

Please come to the bonfire tho, forreal. Ur my favorite person and I will die if you don't come.

I try not to blush or smile too hard in case some of the fish are watching. The bonfire in question, though, kind of sucks. Some townie kids throw it every few months at an inlet on the other side of Lost Lake: the nice side, the side that owns all these boats and isn't covered in the weird green sludge I just got on my shoes. There's a fire, obviously, and people from school and s'mores and spiked lemonade or punch or cider. For sure, something will be spiked. It's not really so bad. Except Joseph will probably be there, and I try my very best to avoid Joseph whenever I can.

Joseph DeLarino.

I scrunch my face up into an expression I immediately change after catching a reflection of it in the water. I don't like being around Joseph if I can help it. We used to date. We don't anymore. He's at all the inlet fires, so for the past several years I haven't been to any, even when we were technically a couple. Rafael said that spoke volumes about the kind of relationship Joseph and I had. I guess he wasn't wrong. But Mei likes going to the inlet fires, and I like Mei, so I've been psyching myself up for a whole week to go to the one tonight. I might back out. I shouldn't. Or maybe I should.

I don't text Mei back. I'll see her soon enough,

anyway. The bus is going to be here in less than ten minutes.

I'm about to turn back to our trailer—it's only in the second row from the lake—but everything is on my mind. Like Mei, and possibly seeing Joseph tonight, and if my dad will feel weird if I come back inside right now, and how I just bailed on Rafael. And I swear all that stuff swirls around me and makes me walk slower, you know? It makes me go in slow motion, all those thoughts; they feel so strong, and kind of stressful. It's like they're keeping me in place. And maybe that's why I see it.

In the lake, out past the green sludge and rotting wooden dock, two misty pink eyes like rose-colored diamonds stare back at me. And they're definitely eyes. Just skimming through the surface of the green water, not even twenty feet away.

If I had met Rafael at the gas station and gotten some of that coffee, I would have dropped it because there are *eyes*. *Pink* eyes. In the *lake*. And they are coming towards me.

I know that's ominous, and I know I should be concerned or scared or *something*. Something besides what I'm actually feeling, because watching those eyes make their way towards me, leaving dark ripples in the water— well, it kind of makes me feel relieved. Saved.

I scramble onto the wooden slats of the green slime-covered docks, as far out as I can go, and grab onto the post at the end. Towards the eyes, not away. It's not about Joseph anymore or the bonfire or worrying about my dad. It's about whatever the hell I'm looking at.

A monster.

I'm crouching down toward the water, holding tightly onto the dock post. The eyes casually look my way. Unblinking. Wild.

I want to say hi. But that doesn't make any sense. I want to see what I'm looking at. It moves closer and just under the water, before it gets too hazy, I can see scales. Shimmery, even though there isn't much sunlight yet to reflect off of them. It's not a fish. It's so much bigger than a fish. I can't see all of it, but that much I can tell. It blinks at me once, and I blink back but vow to never blink again. I might miss something it does.

It—the eyes, the scales, the creature—moves closer. I'm leaning over the water; the wood beneath me is damp and slippery and soft, but I scoot as close to the edge as I can, crouching down with the toes of my Dollar Tree flip-flops over the edge.

I feel wild. I can feel my heartbeat in my fingertips, but it's good. It's the opposite of worrying. It's peace.

It's real. She's real? There's this crazy, quiet, serene sort of monster floating in Lost Lake (the scuzzy end!) and looking up at me with wide, amazing, *real* eyes. And everything is calm. Everything is like a held breath. Like a break from everything crazy in life.

I open my mouth like I have to say something, but before I can, the monster flashes and whips around and I do it—I accidently blink. When I look out at the water again, all that is left is this silvery-orange fin flicking water my way, diving deeper than I can see. Diving away.

I don't know what to do. I don't think I even move for

a solid minute. I don't think I could if I tried. Frozen. That's how the eyes left me. Which isn't great because the bus will be here any minute and I'm still wearing cut-off flannel pajama shorts. I know what I saw was real. I can feel that it was. Because my breath is gone, but in a good way. My head is spinning.

"Callie!" I hear my dad and his voice shatters some kind of trance.

My dad is real, just like the monster in the lake. My dad is real. And he's outside, standing between Javon Jones' trailer and a beginning-to-sprout-leaves oak tree. Dad is half-dressed for work, wearing slacks and a Fleetwood Mac t-shirt, both of which are too big for him.

"Did you eat breakfast?" I hear myself call back. Which is surprising, because I'm usually not so forward with this kind of thing—the eating kind of thing. But I guess most mornings, I don't encounter bold and monstrous creatures in Lost Lake.

He nods and just says, "You need to get dressed, come on." There's a little bit of a laugh in his voice, which is comforting. We don't ever really fight, my dad and I, but eating makes everything a little tense. And laughing makes everything a little better.

"I just saw the weirdest thing," I tell him as I brush by him to get to our porch, and to be honest, I don't know why I say that. I don't know how I think I'm going to explain what I just saw to anyone. But the adrenaline of it is pushing me to talk. Ask almost anyone in my class, they'll tell you I'm pretty quiet, but that's just not true. At school, I'm very bored, like, all the time. But the second anything interesting happens (at school, this is never the case), I don't shut up and I can feel how quickly I get annoying.

And I think I just saw a sea monster. Well, a lake monster. In our backyard. I might not shut up for days.

"What's that?" my dad asks. He's humoring me. He's a good dad, you know? He humors me. He's white, pretty pale (office job), and has a beard that's really scruffy right now. I've got the same pale skin and mousy brown hair that he's got, but my hair is longer, prone to tangling in the most unfortunate ways. My eyes are also darker—dark brown. I think they're like my mom's, but I've never asked.

He follows me inside. *Inside* is pretty cozy. My room is at one end of our place and my dad's is at the other. Somehow there's a kitchen, a bathroom, and a living room shoved in between.

"I don't know how to explain it," I yell from my room. I swap out the flannel shorts for jeans, but I don't think I've got the time to exchange the *Pulp Fiction* shirt I slept in last night with something else. I don't even really like *Pulp Fiction*.

I'm running out the door the next second because even though I can't hear the bus from here, I'm imagining the sounds of it pulling up and away. As I walk out, I try to casually glance at the kitchen table. Half a piece of toast is sitting on Dad's plate. There was only one whole piece of toast to begin with.

"Hey," my dad calls from the sink before I leave. "About this morning."

He turns around, dish rag still in hand, and when he looks at the kitchen table, he tries to be casual, too. But there's half a piece of toast between *us* and *casual*. We've had this conversation before. We've had this morning before. The one where he can hardly bring himself to look at whatever food is in front of him. Where it's tense and awkward and neither of us knows what the hell to say.

So, without meaning to, at the same time, we go with the default:

"Some days are bad days."

Dad smiles, but it's a little bit heartbreaking. That's what his doctors said to him and to me. Some days are going to be bad days.

That's a fact. That's real.

I don't want to leave now. This feels like an open end. Like an opportunity for a spiral. This isn't really an uphill-from-here situation. He'll feel guilty, so he won't eat, then he'll feel even worse, so he'll keep not eating. A never-ending cycle.

"Can you text me when..."

"I'll text you at lunch," he says. "Terry will too," he adds before I can request it.

Terry from work. Dad's friend (I'm sure they're into each other, literally so sure). Terry from work keeps Michael Catwell accountable. She's my peace of mind.

"Okay."

"What were you saying you saw out there?" he asks.

And it all hits me again. The eyes, the monster, the *magic*. And it's all too big and too strange to explain and holy shit, what time is it?

"I'm going to miss the bus."

"*You* text *me* then," he calls as I race out onto the loose stones of the road. I can see the bus pulling up and as the gravel crunches under my shoes, I take one last look at the lake and imagine the monster. She was there, I tell myself. She was magic, and she was real.

2

COFFEE AND BRUISES

THE BUS DRIVER glares at me as I step on the bus, and she lets the doors begin to hiss shut behind me before both my feet have a chance to make it onto the stairs. Which is fair; she was pulling away as I ran up to the door. As I climb in, she hits the gas, and we screech forward, prompting me to hike awkwardly down the aisle of beige seats and too-loud middle schoolers.

"You stood me up, you white bastard!"

Ah, Rafael.

Rafael Vega is one of those people I've known forever, even though we only really started hanging out once we got to high school. He lives at Lake View, like me, but his place is back up against the other end, at the bottom of a rocky drop-off scattered with trees. I like Rafael. Not everyone does. He's kind of a lot.

I make my way to our seat near the back. Rafael is basically standing on the squeaky nylon cushion, and I can feel the bus driver just waiting for him to give her a reason to yell at us. Rafael's got his neon green bandana tied like a headband around his crazy curls, like he always does. I'm not sure where he got it. The bandana. It's very old and very ugly and Rafael wears it every day. He's got on these torn up jeans and a muscle tank that he *will* get in trouble for wearing to school. There are doodles all over his arms and on the little patches of light brown skin that show through his pants. Fading pen tattoos of everything from shooting stars to killer robots to little Puerto Rican flags (and like, a not-unnoticeable amount of genitalia, which I have to assume was the doing of one of his friends). Rafael's parents moved to Lost Lake from Puerto Rico before he was born, and he's always wanted to go back.

I nudge my shoulder into his. "Sorry." And I actually really am. I'm always at least a little bit worried about Rafael when he's at work.

Martin's All-Night Gas and Grub is the gas station convenience store he works at. He takes care of the "All-Night" part, which is concerning because even though we live in a pretty safe town, Raf and I are on the sketchy side of it, and gas stations at two am anywhere don't really scream security. He says he needs the cash, though. I understand money problems. Well, maybe not like he does, but I understand in whatever capacity I can. My dad only has the one job now. Only a couple years ago, though, he was working three. And I'm scheduled most weeknights at a little sandwich shop in town. *In town* sounds better than *all night*.

"Better you and me than you and Joseph," Rafael says, and I try not to wince. I also try to make it look like I didn't hear him. For now, he plays along, but I'm not sure how long that will last. Talking about Joseph with Rafael makes me want to curl up in a ball against this gross bus seat and never have another conversation again.

When Raf talks about Joseph, it's never anything good. And I hate talking shit about people I'm close to, even if maybe there's plenty of shit to talk. Mei always thought Rafael was jealous of us or something, but I don't think that's it. Rafael just doesn't trust Joseph; I never really understood why.

"Well, hey." He graciously moves on, but I still feel uneasy. "If you're willing to sacrifice a hike up a gravel hill to hang out with me, your morning must have been pretty exciting."

At first, I just picture that half-eaten piece of toast probably still sitting out on the kitchen table, and yeah, I guess that was exciting. The bad kind. But then that pair of pinkish-gray eyes come back to me, and suddenly I'm absolutely buzzing.

And Rafael is here. Which means I'm about to sound crazy in front of him.

"I saw a sea monster, Raf." I try to play it off kind of funny, like I'm joking around.

Rafael nods and frowns at me like he's truly willing to believe this. "Out by the lake? Our lake?"

"Not by it. In it. Like the Loch Ness monster or some-thing." And then, after a second, I add, "I'm actually seri-ous. Does that sound wild? I definitely saw something out there."

He sits up in the seat and cranes his neck around like he can maybe catch a glimpse of the monster, even though we're several miles away from Lake View right now.

"You think there's a lake monster? Behind Lake View?"

I just nod and sip my coffee. I can't hear myself talk about this. It sounds crazy, right? It sounds crazy.

But Rafael thinks about it for a second, and really squints out the back window. "Well, there is some weird stuff around here."

A lot of people think along those lines. Lost Lake is a hot spot for weird stuff, and about half of the people that live here will tell you so. I think it's because of the labs where my dad works. They're pretty secretive about some stuff over there, so people make up all these conspiracies: superhumans walking among us, real Bigfoot sightings, plants that'll keep you awake for days if you eat them. Everyone around here has a rumor or two. Rafael has about ninety.

My dad insists they're not true. One time I told him that if the Labs were hiding gigantic secrets, the secretary is the last person they'd tell. He just said, "Secretaries know everyone's secrets. It's right there in the name!" and took a bite of pizza. That was a good day—he actually ate two whole slices while we watched Jurassic Park (thanks, Spielberg).

But for the first time, I'm wondering if there really is something to those rumors. Rafael is right. If I did see what I think I saw—a giant, silvery lake monster—then Lost Lake would have been the place to see it. Unbeliev-able is our thing, right?

"I'm gonna try and see it again," I say, definitively. If

there's a monster in our lake, I've got to find it. If there's something weird lurking around here—science, magic, whatever—I'm already a part of it.

"Gotta get you a boat," Rafael says. "Yo. Jones has one! Crappy little green thing! We should take it out."

"Yeah?"

"Yeah, he likes me." He collapses back against the seat, and his face looks all proud because Mr. Jones doesn't like anyone. The reason he does like Rafael is probably because last year, when some middle schoolers spray painted a bunch of gross stuff on his mailbox, Rafael told them off for half an hour. Rafael is intimidating because his fire never runs out. He could go weeks and months and years without stopping. He's always moving. Like right now—he's tied and untied his bandana about three times since I've gotten on the bus. Honestly, I don't think I've ever seen Rafael sitting down without twirling a pen through his fingers or bouncing his knee up and down within the first five minutes. The kid is made of energy, and it always shows.

"What about tomorrow morning?" I lean my head back on the cracking leather seat, and I can feel the vibrations from the road beneath us shooting around in my skull. "Wanna go out on the lake with me?"

"Aw, Callie, are you finally asking me out?" He bops my nose with his finger, which is incredibly patronizing and also makes the younger kids sitting across from us giggle. But there's something on his arm, so I grab it before he pulls away.

"What the hell?" The underside of his wrist is all purple and blue. Bruised. All the little pen doodles there look like they're floating in outer space. This has happened before. This happens too often. It makes my breathing feel funny—strained and short. And it's not even happening to me.

The kids across from us go, "Ooo!" and make kissing noises, but I don't let go.

"Is this happening? Wow, never in my wildest dreams did I think I'd end up dating Callie Catwell—"

"Shut up." I drop his arm, but I can't get the image out of my head. His arm all dark and purple and menacing. And I know what happened; I do. I know Rafael didn't bump into the shelves at work or trip coming down the road. I know what this is, but still, I ask, "What happened?"

He doesn't say anything for a few seconds, which I hate, because Rafael and silence never go together. It kind of confirms what I'm thinking.

"Kyle?" I ask Rafael quietly.

"Yeah, whatever, Kyle." Rafael turns his arm over and rolls his eyes so far back that he's looking out the window.

Kyle is Raf's mom's boyfriend. I've only seen him a few times, even though he's probably been around for over a year. A real shady white guy that sulks around and always looks like he only got dressed halfway. My stomach is all knotted up. I side-eye Rafael's bruise. I swear it got worse when I looked away.

I know he doesn't want me to say what I'm about to say. And maybe that means I shouldn't say it. But I also can't shake the feeling that I should, and I feel shitty for not knowing either way. So when I say, "Stay at our place,

Raf," it comes out really quiet and timid, and I hope he knows that I mean it.

But he just says, "No, Callie. No way." Like he always does, every time.

He stays at his trailer, with his mom and gross-Kyle, backed into the forested hill that surrounds our little neighborhood. It's kind of like the trees there absorb all of the noise and hurt and pain.

"What happened?"

"He just— I don't know, Callie! He thought I was sneaking out or something when I was leaving for work. He just freaks out sometimes," Rafael says, facing the scratched-up bus window, wanting to change the subject. "There's nothing I can do about it." And it sounds wrong coming out of his mouth. Like it's hurting him to say it.

I hate this. Because, well, obviously.

It feels like there are a million things I can do to help Rafael and, at the same time, absolutely none. One time, I suggested that we tell his mom, but he just told me *she gets it worse* and then totally shut down. And I hate it. But that's not exactly helpful.

Rafael punches the seat in front of us, maybe just for something to do, and then he says, "Yeah. Let's go on the lake tomorrow morning. If there's a monster in our back-yard, I wanna get credit for finding it."

Change the subject, move on, keep going. I don't know if it's what we should do, and I don't think either of us are really over the fact that this was a conversation we had. But we fist bump on the boat thing like a pair of middle school boys, and I figure that a morning out on the lake is better than a morning in the same vicinity as Kyle.

We talk about conspiracy theories for the rest of the bus ride, which maybe isn't the best avoidance technique, but after a while, Rafael starts to seem more like himself. More animated and goofy and wild, and it's crazy how insanely *not* himself he was when we were talking about Kyle. It's crazy the kind of shift that I can see.

Rafael is a good guy. He's my favorite guy, and I'm excited that he's excited about this maybe-hallucination of a lake monster that I saw. So, when I text Mei about what I think I saw, it's against my better judgment. Just like when I started to mention the monster to my dad. I'm excited, swept up in the buzz of it all, and I forget that maybe I sound crazy.

I send *I got crazy news!!!*, ignoring her question from before about the inlet bonfire.

And she immediately sends back *I can't wait to hear it cutie* with a million pink hearts.

By the time we get to school, Raf and I have covered the more nuanced arguments regarding the validity of all of the bigfoot sightings around here. We both want them to be true, though, so it's not exactly an impartial discussion. We don't talk about Kyle again or whatever happened to Rafael last night. We also don't talk about Joseph, which I'm incredibly grateful for.

When Rafael pulls on the red Adidas hoodie he's had for years, I don't mention that it's starting to get kind of hot and I don't mention the bruises on his arms or stupid Kyle again. I might think about it all day, but that's on me. I'll also be thinking about the lake monster and going to the bonfire and trying not to see Joseph there. I might think about Mei, and how she just called me *cutie* (it's in writing), and how that probably means nothing but could possibly mean *something*.

As we're climbing out onto the sidewalk, Rafael calls, "What's up, mofos!" and a bunch of people roll their eyes, but a few people say "ayyeee!" and Raf smiles, and I'm just thinking he deserves better. He really does. And then we walk inside and have to go to school.

3

TRAILER TRASH

MEI IS MY BEST FRIEND. And yeah, she's incredibly beautiful. I am beyond serious, and you would get it if you ever met and/or saw her. Mei is beautiful like sunrises and landscapes and the puffs of clouds that rise off of the lake on sunny mornings. She's impossible to look away from because she is mesmerizing. She's happening now.

She is the epitome of kind and friendly and sociable, and I'm not totally sure how we're friends because I am probably the opposite of all that. Not that I'm a total asshole or anything (I mean, hopefully not). It's just kind of difficult to be nice to people if you don't hang out with too many of them. But Mei hangs out with everyone, even Rafael, despite how she thinks he's wild. She makes whoever she's with feel totally at ease. Sometimes I swear I can feel her walking into a room before I even see her. You don't want to miss her. People just relax when she's around. It's incredible.

Right now, she's coming down the hallway with all of the dance girls. They've been here since six-thirty for dance team, of which Mei is the captain. She's still in her leotard with sweatpants pulled over it, and when she spots me, she rushes a bit ahead of the group.

"Oh my God," she squeals. The hallway isn't packed yet, but a few people still look her way. "Callie, Callie, Callie!" She tugs at my arm, and being near her honestly makes my skin feel all warm. She says, "I've got weird news."

I'm smiling. I always am when I see her and see that she's excited to see me. Mutual excitement. Someone excited because of me? Wild. Incredible. Of course I'm smiling.

But she has weird news? "I thought that was me."

"We both have weird news now. We're pretty in sync like that." She throws her arm around me and we're walking together towards my locker like some kind of four-legged monster. Which I'm fine with. Her dark hair is in a messy-ish bun and her bangs, which she tried to pin back, are falling in wisps all across her face.

She leans in even closer to me and whispers, "What's your news? Mine is pretty wild."

And I laugh. Not even sure why. I just laugh, because she's right up against me and her bangs are all crazy and her bun is slipping out, and she's just always something magical. Like the lake monster, like my news.

"Uh…" This is the part where all of my excitement catches up to me. This is where I realize I spoke too soon about something I was too hyped up about and now I'm kind of embarrassed to say anything at all. It's like relaying a joke you heard when you were tired and delirious to a group of people who are wide awake. It won't land. It won't feel like it did in the moment. There will be a dissonance between *now* and *then*.

I think maybe I made a mistake.

But before I can mumble anything together, I hear behind us: "She saw a lake monster!"

Mei straightens up and turns around. "Rafael?" And of course he's there, surrounded by all his buddies, because this is what he does every morning: collects his entourage then comes to find me, because I've probably found Mei, and if Mei is around, that means her brother, Jian, might show up. I'm almost positive Rafael is in love with Jian.

"Mei," Raf nods suavely.

And Mei turns back to me, "Is he serious?"

"Oh." I guess I hadn't expected her to accept it, not so suddenly. Not from Raf. "Yeah. I think so."

"A lake monster?" She lets go of my shoulders and leans against the lockers next to mine as I exchange a few books.

"I know that sounds dumb—"

"No," Mei says. "I believe you." My stomach flutters. "I was just thinking... Around here? That makes sense."

"That's what I was saying!" Rafael says. His entourage agrees and Mei nods at him approvingly and something inside of me relaxes. I love it when they get along, even about crazy, ridiculous things like this, like a monster in Lost Lake.

Rafael continues, "You know they were saying how there was that giant wolf wandering around in the woods last year? It's like that."

"That was made up."

I glance beside me and there is Jian, standing by Mei's shoulder.

They're twins, but they're complete opposites. Mei is all curves and smiles and extracurriculars. Jian is like one of those cryptids he's so sure don't exist. The hidebehind. Tall and lurking and a total myth to some people. Their parents met one month after they both moved here from the same town in China. Jian looks more like their mom, Mei like their dad.

Jian is a nerd but not in the good-grades way. Mei told me he's basically failing his history class. He's a nerd in the awkwardly-unable-to-talk-to-anyone way—basically in the same way as me. We're very similar, and that is probably why, even though for the past six years Mei and I have basically been inseparable, Jian and I have hardly spoken to each other at all. I kind of wish we were better friends, but at this point, it feels weird to even approach that. He knows all the good hiking spots around here, though.

And he's absolutely terrified of Rafael.

Rafael leans against the wall next to Jian, and all his friends give him solemn nods and thumbs up from the opposite end of the hallway. "Jian, what's good, mofo!" To most people, that would sound mean. But that's just because they don't realize that Rafael isn't saying mofo ironically. He just genuinely thinks that's a normal way to talk. He's as awkward as the rest of us, just way more confident about it.

"Nothing much," Jian mutters. He glances from me to Mei with terrified eyes.

Rafael grabs Jian's shoulder, which is significantly higher than his own. Jian looks horrified.

"You gonna be at the inlet fire tonight?" Rafael asks.

"I don't—"

"You should come!" Rafael slaps Jian on the shoulder and then shoots finger guns his way. "I'll see you there? I'll see you there."

Rafael gets absorbed into his group of friends and they all sling their arms around him like they're a singular entity of mismatching limbs.

"Why does he have to be such a jerk?" Mei's watching as Rafael heads away down the hall, periodically looking back to Jian and then laughing with each other. And I know it looks mean, but I really don't think they're trying to be. In fact, I think they're going for the exact opposite. I think Rafael is trying to flirt and I think his friends think he's doing a great job. It's actually hilarious, because Jian and Mei are from a different world than Rafael and me.

Our world is Lake View Mobile Home Park. It's midnight yelling matches coming from somewhere nearby and thrift shopping out of necessity. Mei and I have been friends for so long that we kind of understand the things that make us different, but I don't think Jian does. Rafael and I were grown in different soil. I can kind of see both sides of this, though.

Jian only really knows me because I'm friends with Mei and I'm friends with Mei because some higher force put us in the same homeroom in sixth grade. I've got a view into both of these worlds. I speak both of their languages (well, not *really*, Jian and Mei can actually speak a different language. Mandarin. I'm in level two Spanish, though).

Bottom line is that in the ridiculous saga of Jian and Rafael's relationship, I know what's going on. Probably way more than anyone else does. Including Jian and Rafael. If Rafael is hopelessly smitten with Jian, he demonstrates his feelings by knocking into his shoulder every time they pass in the hallway and yelling profanities at him. Which just isn't super effective, or, at least, it hasn't been so far.

But Rafael is good, and I can kind of see him and Jian together. Rafael isn't one to mess around with people. His mom and dad are separated and on good terms from what I've heard. But Raf's dad isn't ever around. He doesn't really communicate with Raf or his mom on a regular basis, and I think Rafael kind of hates that. One time, when we were maybe kind of tipsy on Raf's mom's sangria, Rafael told me, "You keep the people you love in your life, no matter what. If you don't—I don't know. How can you even know that they love you?"

I guess I just know that Rafael is a good one. And even though Jian and I aren't close, I'm pretty sure he is too. They're different, but isn't everyone? Isn't that good? I think them being together isn't as absurd as anyone would initially think.

"Here." Jian hands Mei an envelope of lunch money and I'm about to ask if he *is* going to be at the bonfire tonight (expert wing woman?), when I feel someone's hand around my waist.

"Hey, trailer trash."

Joseph DeLarino's voice rumbles in my ear and I feel a

little sick. I push his hand away and turn around, but he's still right in my space. "Don't call me that."

"Don't ignore my texts."

Joseph DeLarino stands before me with his dark curls and darker eyelashes. His skin is so white and so pale and so clear that everyone in middle school called him a vampire. I'm not sure when people changed their minds and decided he was super attractive, but that's the general consensus now. He works out, a fact he brings up just this side of too often. He can charm anyone, even the teachers, into liking him. We used to date, though, and I can see when he's doing it—*manipulating*. Smirking and winking and *leaning* in front of my locker so I can't get my gym bag out. And I'm pretty much focused on him because I always am when he's anywhere near me, but a little spot in the back of my head is reserved for Rafael and how I'm glad he just walked away. He always gets really passive aggressive around Joseph. Joseph always calls him on it. It's the worst.

Mei shifts beside me, straightening her shoulders and lifting her chin just slightly, just noticeably—dancer posture—and it makes Joseph back off a bit. I'm not sure how she does it, but Joseph's always been a little bit terrified of Mei, and it's one of my favorite things to watch happen.

Joseph is right about the texts, though. I haven't responded to anything he's sent me in days. I don't know what he's trying to do or why he's wasting time on me. Like he thinks I'm playing hard to get, making him work for something.

But I don't want something with Joseph DeLarino. With him, I want absolutely nothing at all.

I realize I haven't actually said anything to him, just thought a lot of things and grabbed awkwardly between Joseph and my locker for my gym bag. He's looking at me, half a smile on his lips and dark shadows over his eyes.

Mei slides between us and waves her hand in my face, "Heyo. Callie Cat. We've got things to talk about."

She drags my hand with my gym bag away from my locker and slams the door shut, pulling me towards the locker rooms down the hallway. I think Joseph calls something out, but I don't really hear him.

"What a dick," Mei mutters, shouldering into the locker room. "You didn't actually want to talk to him, right? I didn't just pull you away from some epic get-back-together moment?"

"No, definitely not." Definitely, definitely not.

"Good." Mei swings her gym locker open and her duffle bag tumbles out, spilling dance shoes and t-shirts all over the floor. "You're sure, though?" She speaks to me from behind the red locker door. I hand her a sneaker. I don't really know how to respond.

Honestly? Now I'm not sure. When Joseph and I were together, things weren't great. At least, I don't think they were. I kind of just remember being really nervous and stressed out all the time. He was always into things I wasn't. Like kissing. And more than kissing. We never did anything crazy, or anything I didn't want to do, but I was always waiting for it. I was always waiting for us to finally decide to have sex or something. And even thinking about it now is making me panic. That's why I broke it off

—I didn't want us to have to deal with that. *I* didn't want to deal with that. Not with Joseph.

Mei peaks at me from behind the locker door.

"Uh..." Am I sure I don't want to get back together with Joseph? "Yeah." I think I am.

"You don't sound sure."

"I don't know," I say. I didn't exactly break up with him in the best way. I didn't explain anything to him, and I guess I kind of feel shitty about that, which is why I don't totally ignore his texts. I at least owe him some kind of communication, right? "I guess I just don't really like hanging out with him."

Mei hands me a cardigan from her locker and keeps digging through it. "Then don't."

I fold up a pink shirt and tuck it back onto the locker shelf. "No, yeah. I know." But with Joseph, it's not as simple as just not hanging out with him. There's history there. He was the first person I dated. I can't just totally drop him.

Mei leans out of her locker, a blue shirt in hand, and leans back on her hip, looking down at me. "Did you like dating him?"

"No." The answer is out before I can think about it, but I guess that's okay. I guess it's true. "No, not really."

"You never seemed like yourself when you were together. I mean, like, if you and I hung out after you were out with him? You were different then."

"Really?"

"Yeah." Mei slips out of her leotard and I watch the wall in front of me. "I always thought you could do better."

That makes me laugh. Mei pulls the blue top down over her head. It's one of those strappy ones that give you weird tan lines in the summer but looks amazing. "I'm serious, Callie."

I try not to blush or think too hard about that. "Well, I always thought you could do better than Bryce Hellings."

"Ugh!" She takes the cardigan from me and then throws it into my face. "Everyone in the world can do better than Bryce Hellings. Please don't remind me that that ever happened."

I laugh and toss her sweater back to her. Honestly, doing better than Joseph is kind of hard for me to make sense of. In a lot of ways, Joseph wasn't even on my radar. I mean, we were a couple, so obviously I was aware of him but... I don't know. I'm not even sure how we started dating. It just kind of happened. I just kind of let it all happen. It was a routine with him. It was just a thing I thought I had to do. Date a boy. It made me nervous and stressed and sometimes terrified. Our relationship was never something I wanted to make a big deal about.

I can't do better than Joseph. Especially since I didn't really want to do anything with him in the first place. But he's still in my life and I still don't really know what to do about it. He's going to be at the bonfire. Ugh.

"About tonight—"

The bell rings and cuts me off. What's the opposite of saved by the bell? Inhibited from getting out of going to a party by the bell. Mei looks up at the clock. "Crap. Do you have bobby pins?"

I pat down my pockets until I find a few, which are all

hers. I find them scattered around at home anytime she's there and I always try to have some on me.

"Life saver." Mei somehow manages to pin back any fly-aways and bumps in less than two seconds, which I'm convinced is some kind of secret dancer skill. Then she turns to me and frowns. "Rafael mentioned a lake monster?"

"You mentioned weird news?"

"Yes!" Mei throws various shoes and articles of clothing haphazardly in her locker and I try to organize them as they fall in. "I can drive you home today. We can talk then?"

"Yeah, okay."

"You all right, Callie?"

"All good, all good." Though all I can hear in my head is *trailer trash* in Joseph's voice. And all I can feel is his hand on my waist. Bleh. I back up towards the door and try to get Joseph DeLarino out of my head. "I'll meet you here then?"

"Love it."

"Love it." I push my way out into the hallway. "Bye!"

4

TERRY FROM WORK

I'M NOT great at school. Mostly, I'm bored, so mostly, I don't really focus on anything I need to for more than a few minutes. But that's whatever. I get by with B's and C's. There are more interesting and worrisome things to have on my mind than anything that could possibly be happening in statistics class. Like Terry from work.

She sends me a text as I'm sitting down for statistics and it relaxes me a bit.

Finished our lunch break. Now back to work!

Then a message comes through from my dad. Just a photo. It's him and Terry, flexing in front of his desk. Terry has her orange hair tied into a long braid and she's holding the end of it under her nose like a mustache against pale white skin. I make sure to save it because it's very embarrassing for both of them, honestly, and also one of my favorite things I've ever seen.

All of this seems like a good sign, but I still don't know what he ate. Terry would have told me if something was off.

I'm not sure when my dad started being friends with Terry, but he talks about her a lot, and she knows about his eating disorder.

Which is weird.

I mean honestly, *I* hardly know about his eating disorder. My dad and I get along really well and I always thought we were pretty open with each other. I don't keep much from him, and I don't need to. Usually.

So I was surprised by it all. That's it. Just surprised. Because for as open as it seemed like we were, I didn't know what to do when he dropped the news. I was a freshman two years ago when he got the diagnosis and told me that he was going for treatment. They tell you what anorexia is in school. We know about it and we know it exists and that it's dangerous, and we have an understanding of who it usually affects. So I guess I just thought, if anyone was supposed to develop a hatred of food, it was supposed to be me.

But it was Michael Catwell, and I didn't know what to do, or what I could do.

At first, I thought it was a little weird that Terry from work knew about his anorexia when I'd lived with him for my entire life and had still completely missed it. But once I got over the strangeness of it all (and maybe I haven't, not totally), having Terry in the know has actually been a good thing. For Dad and for me, because, well, she's Terry from work. Which means she sees my dad *at work*. Which means that I don't have to freak out about whether or not my dad is lying to me about what he ate all day. And I hate myself a little bit more every time I think like this, worried that he's lying. It's not that I don't trust him; it's just that I don't even think he trusts himself.

I may be pulling B's and C's now, but when I first learned about what was going on with my dad, I was hard-core failing every class. That doesn't happen so much now that Terry gave me her number.

I slip my phone into my bag and try not to think about the two of them at work right now. I hate being pushy about this. I feel like I make everything worse with my own brand of crazy.

Maybe she didn't say anything because things *are* bad. Maybe, maybe, maybe.

Shit.

I pull my phone back out. I type out *Did he eat most of the stuff in his lunch?* and let my thumb hover over the send button as chairs start to fill up around me, the sound of desks scraping against linoleum and backpacks being zipped open buzzing around my ears.

In the corner of my eye, I see ratty, torn-up jeans standing by me. I hit send. I look up. Rafael and I have statistics together, which makes it a little more bearable. When he catches my eye and bares his teeth at me in a creepy smile, it's easy not to worry about how much I'm texting Terry or if I should regret sending that last message.

Rafael is pretty good at commanding attention. He sits down but doesn't really stop moving, and the first thing he says to me is, "Yo, do you think Jian is mad at me?" I try not to laugh or roll my eyes.

"No."

"Okay, okay." Rafael settles into his seat and I notice

that he's still got his hoodie on, even though everyone else has shed whatever layers they could; we don't have air conditioning in here and April makes things pretty humid. "It just seemed like maybe he was."

I tell him, "You make him nervous."

"What? Why?"

"I don't know. You just..." I wave my hand around in the air by Rafael and try to find the words. They're just different. They just don't get each other. At least, not right now. "You have an intense energy."

"Psh!" Rafael swats at me and collapses into a slouch, facing the front of the classroom. "Intense energy my ass. What does that even mean? Intense energy."

I don't know how to describe it. I don't. But I try. "You're a nice person, but it's like you want people to think you're a mean person."

"I'm not nice," he says immediately, like it's something he's sure of. And I don't get that at all.

"...Um, yeah. You really are."

Raf looks like he wants to fight it, but the bell rings and our teacher picks up right away.

I half pay attention for the rest of class and subtly glance at my phone a few times, but nothing ever comes back from Terry. Maybe she's pissed at me. Not pissed. That doesn't seem like her. Annoyed, though. She could be annoyed and too nice to say anything about it. Damn. All these nice people. I manage to refrain from sending her anything else, even though I want to.

Someone pokes me in the side, and I flinch so hard that I drop my pen. I look over and it's only Rafael trying to hand me a folded-up piece of paper. I snatch it from him and try not to let it crinkle too loudly as I unfold the note.

It's scrawled out, *Who are you texting under the table?*

I write back *No one. Pay attention.*

Joseph?

Seeing that makes my chest feel like ice. Instead of writing back, I look up to Raf. His eyebrows are raised, but his eyes are fierce. Some kind of weird challenge. I scowl and shake my head.

I think he's about to snatch the paper back from me, but the teacher says his name, fast and sharp, and asks Rafael a question. Somehow, he answers with ease (which I certainly would not have been able to do) and I try to avoid making eye contact with him for the rest of class. And look, I get that Rafael is concerned about me. I mean, I think I get it. But I don't really understand *why*. Joseph and I were bad together. That's it. Why does he act like there's more to it than that?

Even though Terry didn't respond to my last message, I send her another one. Just a question mark. Which immediately feels pushy, but I'm so on edge right now, I can hardly find space in my consciousness to worry about it. I know I'm being overbearing, but if I'm going to get called out for texting, I might as well actually text.

At the end of class, I have to awkwardly ask Camila Flores to walk me through some of the practice problems, since I definitely wasn't paying attention, and I don't want to ask Raf for help and end up talking about Joseph. Camila is nice enough, but in that cool and intimidating way that makes me think there is way more to her than she's letting on. She's undeniably good at joint probability distribution, though.

Camila and I don't talk much outside of class. In fact, we don't talk much inside of class, so she surprises me when she asks, "You know Mei pretty well, right?"

"Mei Huang?" I say stupidly.

She chuckles. Effortless. Cool. "Yeah. Her."

"Um..." I look at Camila, trying to read her, but it's kind of difficult. Her expression is just on the interested side of neutral. She looks invested in this conversation but not *too* invested. With long fingers, she ruffles her dark curls over one shoulder. I blink. "Yeah. Yeah, we're pretty close."

"Thought so," Camila says, glancing back down at her notes. I'm wondering if maybe our conversation is over but then, without looking up, she says, "Tell her I said hi."

And I have no idea what the hell that's all about, so I just say, "Right, yeah, sure."

When the bell rings, I check my messages. There's something from Joseph, which makes me antsy, but I ignore it. Terry texted me back.

Callie, it took a while but he got through the cucumbers and some of that sandwich. It's not the best but he did get some food in him! There are going to be bad days but it'll be okay!

I run into the doorway on the way out because I'm reading and re-reading that last line over and over. I don't know why, but I really wasn't expecting to see it in a text from Terry. *There are going to be bad days.* Does Terry get to say that now, too? And is this really all just a bad day? It seemed to me Dad had been doing much better recently until this morning, but maybe not. Maybe I'm missing them again—all the warning signs.

I want to text my dad, but I don't want to overwhelm him. I want to leave school, but I can't afford to miss any class time. I want to go back to this morning and stay inside during breakfast, instead of wandering out to the lake and reevaluating everything that happened between Dad and me. We didn't leave off on a great note. Maybe I should have stayed. Maybe it would have been worth it to miss the bus and a bit of the school day. Maybe.

"Aye, C," Rafael says, bumping his shoulder into mine.

"Raf!"

"I see you trying to swerve me, girl."

"No! Never." Except maybe right now, yeah. Just a bit.

"I know you don't like to talk about Joseph—"

Here we go. "That's not it—"

"No, that's the problem! You don't want to talk about him. Callie." He slides in front of me so both of us stop making forward progress down the hallway.

I make my eyes all buggy and wide. "Rafael."

"I'm sorry if this is coming off all... I don't know, protective and judge-y."

"It is coming off that way."

"I'm sorry. That guy is just a douchebag and you can do better than him and if you guys are going to get back together, that's cool—"

"We're not!"

"Well, okay then. Just," Rafael scratches at the back of his neck and watches all the people navigating around us, "be careful with him, you know?"

Be careful with him. You can do better than him.

Joseph is annoying, not dangerous. And he's a boy that talks to me sometimes, not my last hope at love in this world. I don't get how Rafael can tell me to be careful around someone like Joseph when he lives with Kyle. I don't get it. But I don't say anything like that. Not right now. I just jerk my head down the hallway and nudge my shoulder into his.

"Let's go."

"Whatever, Callie," he says. But he's smiling and slinging an arm around my shoulder and we walk like that together until we have to part ways. It's nice to have a friend holding you up, I guess. And when Raf and I separate, I am kind of grateful that he cares enough to worry. More than grateful. I think I'm pretty lucky.

The text from Joseph still sits unread on my phone and it feels like a weight dragging down my backpack, making it stupidly difficult to continue on down the hallways alone.

I wonder if that's how it is with Dad and Terry. With Dad and me. I wonder if Dad feels lucky to have us. I wonder if we make any of what he's going through any easier. Or maybe, some days are just bad days, regardless of who's in them.

5

I LEARN THINGS ABOUT CAMILA FLORES

MEI and I don't have a single class together this semester, which is an absolute travesty, (her words, my thoughts) but I see her more than I see almost anyone else. She takes and teaches dance lessons in the studio called Beetle's Dance, above the sandwich shop, Joey's Sandwiches, where I work. She's got a car—a dark number I don't know the make and model of—so we usually leave everywhere together and then hang out for stupid amounts of time watching stupid amounts of YouTube and Netflix.

I'm waiting in that nameless car right now, listening to the slight whistle of the wind outside and scrolling through all the messages I've gotten from Joseph in the past week. They're all kind of flirty. All kind of gross. He knows we broke up, right?

"Catwell!" Mei smushes her face against the driver's side window and knocks frantically at me before climbing in, and all of the tension that's been building up inside of me all day gets pushed away to the back of my brain. "Hey."

"Hi." I grab her dance bag from her and throw it in the back.

"You ready for this fire?"

"Ugh." It's just us now, which makes it easier to stop pretending I haven't been dreading it all day. "No."

The inlet bonfires are kind of a big deal around here. Like school dances, plus alcohol, minus teachers. A lot of the girls get all dressed up and a lot of the boys put on slightly nicer t-shirts than they had on all day. It's a whole thing. A whole lot of effort.

But Mei will be there. And probably Rafael too. Plus, my dad isn't going to be home until later tonight, and if I'm sitting around in my room until then, I might go a little crazy.

Mei pokes my cheek. "You'll be fine." She's probably right.

Probably.

Once we get to my place, I hop in the shower and Mei sits on the plastic seat cover of the toilet and talks through the curtain. This is just how we hang out sometimes.

"You know there are people who are like physical therapists but specifically for dancers?"

"I did not." I make the water a bit colder so that the steam doesn't build up too much. I try to recall any and all information I've ever heard about dance physical therapists and come up empty.

"Well, that's kind of my plan now," Mei tells me. "Physical therapist but for dancers."

I peek my eyes out from behind the curtain. "That's really cool." And it is.

Unlike me and unlike her brother, Mei is pretty good at school. When she took the PSATs freshman year, she completely aced them, which is impressive because freshmen aren't even supposed to be taking the PSATs.

Mei has always been smart, and I think it's because she genuinely likes to learn things. All things. Any things. It's kind of awesome. She's just constantly reading about, or working on, or crazy-studying whatever is going on in her life. Mei goes all in—her life is so fast paced, and I don't know how she does it. School and parties and football games and *engaging* with life. She's so engaged all the time. I feel like I can't keep up with her, but somehow, the two of us just work.

So yeah, Mei is shamelessly nerdy about many things. Dance most of all, but also all of her science classes, which is awesome because I don't think I've remembered anything from a science class since I've started taking science classes. She ends up worrying about college and grades and all of that, but she really doesn't need to. I'm really sure she's going to be okay.

"I don't know, though," she says on the other side of the curtain. "I kind of feel like it's a made-up career."

"Doesn't sound made-up." I duck back under the water. "It actually sounds kind of perfect."

"Oh!" Mei must have sat up because I can hear some of the bottles on the shelf behind the toilet rattle together. "You'll never guess what happened today."

"Is this your weird news?" I'd almost forgotten she even had weird news, which feels selfish and stupid.

There's too much to get swept up in. My mind has been shuffling around all day. It does that every day. There's too much to focus on, so I think I try to focus on it all at once, which has proven to be grossly ineffective.

"Callie!"

"What?" I've done it again. Zoned out. A million different tangents live in my brain.

"Tell me what you remember me saying."

Mei has to ask that a lot. It's another dumb thing my head does. I'll hear something and realize I heard it on a delay. Mei and my dad really don't even repeat themselves anymore, they just wait for me to catch up. I'm sure that I'm crazy.

But I do remember. Just a few seconds ago. "You were talking about Camila Flores, right?" Camila Flores, from statistics.

"Yes! Camila Flores. This morning, she showed up at the end of dance rehearsal and, oh my God, Callie..." A long pause. I don't move. I lean in towards the curtain. Mei says, very quietly, "She asked me to *prom*!"

She what?! "She *what?!*" I stick my head out of the shower and internally cringe at the little puddle created by the dripping mess of my hair.

"I know!"

"Like as a date?" The plastic curtain crinkles in my grip.

"Like a full-on, what-color-is-your-dress-'cause-I-have-to-get-you-a-corsage date."

"I didn't know she was—I didn't know you were—"

"Neither did I!" Mei slumps back against the shelf and

a little bottle of lotion clatters onto her lap. "Ugh, I just don't know what to do."

She takes a deep breath and I panic for a second because this is where I should say something, right? This is where I should have a level head, balance her out. And I'm not there yet.

Thankfully, Mei goes on. "Wow, okay. It's good to say that out loud. Holy shit, I don't even know what to think right now!" She fiddles with a loose strand of hair and cuts her eyes to me. "Maybe I'm overreacting. What's the big deal, right? It's not a big deal." She presses a hand over her heart. "It kind of feels like a big deal."

It definitely, definitely does. I duck back into the shower because I can feel the warm water running out, but my mind stays outside with Mei. I think I kind of expected someone to be pregnant or be cheating on their boyfriend. Or finding a lake monster.

But Camila Flores? Asking Mei to prom? It makes my stomach feel funny and I don't know why. I lean against the slippery tile of the shower wall and let the water cascade over my fingers. This wasn't what I expected. This wasn't something I thought would happen. I need to say something, I really do. But I don't know what makes sense to say right now.

"That's, um... What did you tell her?" I ask. I have to force myself to sound casual, which feels like the epitome of *not casual*.

"Well, I didn't tell her anything for like, a full minute! And then I was just like, *wow, Camila, that's so, so sweet. Can I think about it?* And she just kind of laughed, all cool-like and said, *yeah, no pressure girl*, and I was like, *Ahhh!*"

"Ahhh..."

"Callie, like what the hell? What should I even do?"

"Well." I don't know what to tell her. Camila Flores? I only know two things about Camila Flores. One: She moved here with her family from Mexico in the fourth grade, and two: she's into girls, which I just figured out about three seconds ago. "Do you want to go with her?" I ask. And I sound quiet. I know I sound quiet. For a second, I'm worried that the water drowns out my voice because after several moments, Mei still hasn't answered.

But then she says, just as quiet as me, "I don't know. Maybe?" I can hear Mei shift around. I was in the middle of shaving my legs, but that is an effort that I have officially abandoned. "She's... well, she's a *she*. I've never even thought about that."

"Well, that's okay." The water is totally cold now, but I don't move. "Going to prom with a girl doesn't mean you're, like, a lesbian."

"I know. But what if it does mean that? What if I want it to mean that?"

I'm absolutely buzzing. For as much as we talk about everything, we've never talked about *this*. About what kind of people we're into. Mei's only dated a few boys, and she never seemed crazy about any of them—at least, I never thought so. Does she think about guys? Girls? I guess friends talk about this stuff. We never did. That was never a part of our relationship. I'm only now realizing that maybe that isn't normal.

"Do you... want it to mean that?"

"I don't know!" Mei stands up. I can hear her pacing

in the little space that there is in our bathroom. "Would you ever kiss a girl, Callie?"

The question knocks the air out of me, and I suddenly feel dizzy. Would I ever kiss a girl? Truth is, I don't think much about kissing anyone. Mei may have had a few relationships since we've been friends, but I was only in one. With Joseph DeLarino. And all I learned from that whole ordeal was that I'm not really excited about the stuff people are supposed to be excited about. I never really wanted to kiss him, and I don't think I ever liked it when he kissed me. And Joseph was interested in way more than kissing.

"Callie?"

I shut the water off and grab a towel from the hook outside the shower. Would I ever kiss a girl?

"I think so. Yeah."

I wrap the towel around me—it's old and kind of scratchy—and when I push away the curtain, Mei is staring at me with eyebrows arched high. "Really?"

I try not to act like this conversation is a big deal to me, even though it definitely, definitely is. Yes. I would kiss a girl. One particular girl, if she ever wanted me to.

I shoulder by her to get to my room and busy myself with looking through my closet, even though I know what I'm going to wear (cutoff shorts and a giant flannel that is the exact same color as a pumpkin).

"It was just unexpected, is all," Mei says quietly from the bathroom. I can see her fiddling with her bangs in the tiny bathroom mirror and I feel kind of bad, because, if I'm being honest, all of this is unexpected for me too.

I didn't think I seriously had a crush on Mei and I

certainly didn't think that there would be other girls she'd be interested in. But here I am, panicking into the top drawer of my dresser. And there she is, considering dating a girl—that is not me—and having a crisis in our tiny bathroom.

I've only got my shirt halfway buttoned up when Mei slides into my room. It's always been a small room, but I'm really feeling that now. Mei seems unbothered. This is normal. She's been here a million times. What we haven't done a million times is have conversations about crushes and sexuality and kissing. What we haven't done a million times is exist together in the same space, while I can't stop hearing a single word biting at my ears, relentless and wild and magic: *possibility*.

I'm being ridiculous.

"Is, uh—is Camila going to be at the fire tonight?" I ask. I really don't want to think about Mei and Camila, but Mei clearly wants to. She clearly *needs* to.

"Shit, I didn't even think of that!" Mei collapses onto my semi-made bed, puffs of faded blue comforter billowing around her. "Probably, yeah." She rolls to the side and buries her face in one of my pillows. "Ugh! What do I do?"

I sit down beside her, gently, and stare at the floor—gruff, scratchy carpet—until I feel her shifting to sit up beside me. What should she do? I don't even know how to answer. It suddenly seems weird that this wasn't something she's had to deal with before.

"People have asked you out before," I try.

"Yeah. Boys."

"What did you do then?"

"I just... I don't know. This doesn't feel like that." She looks at me, and her expression breaks my heart. Her eyes are wide, but her brows are pinched together. I think she might cry. I grab her hand. "Before, with all those guys, I honestly never cared enough to worry. It's different now. Like, I don't want to mess it up now."

"You're not going to mess anything up," I say. And if I'm confused about everything else at this moment, I'm not confused about that. "You're going to figure it out. We're going to figure it out. It'll be okay." I don't know where any of that comes from, but I guess I definitely believe it. It's easy to be strong for Mei. It's easy to believe the best for her because she is the best. In my life, she's the best. So that's what I'll give her. That's what I'll fight for. The best.

Eventually, softly, Mei says, "Orange looks good on you." She tugs at the sleeve of my shirt. "It looks really bad on basically everyone, but it looks good on you."

"Thanks," I squeak out.

She slides to the floor and my arm feels really cold where hers used to be pressing against it. Mei is sitting in front of the tiny IKEA bookshelf shoved against the foot of my bed. It's where I keep my DVDs. Right now, they're organized by color and nothing else.

"What would your artsy movie kids do, Callie?" she asks. And when I slide down beside her, she wraps an arm around my shoulder. The artsy kid movies are her favorite —all the pretty people and poetic lines. I like that she likes them. It's really sweet.

"Go on a road trip, probably."

"To where?"

"Oh, they'd figure it out along the way."

She laughs, and I laugh, and then we're quiet for a bit. I hear my phone buzz on the other side of the room, but I don't feel like I need to check it right at this moment, and I'm filled with some sort of feeling that is incredibly strange. Because with Mei beside me, even though she's talking about going out with someone else, another girl, I'm not feeling squeamish or uneasy or jealous, even though maybe I was before. It's like I can't feel those things right now. We're just here, together, sitting on the floor and staring at my dumb movie collection like a couple of weirdos.

Eventually, Mei lifts her head up and turns to me. "What was Rafael saying about a lake monster?"

And then I'm laughing again because I don't even know where to begin with that story. The whole thing feels super real and super made up at the same time. I can't believe it happened just this morning.

"Okay, I know this sounds stupid and crazy—"

"It doesn't, actually."

"I'm just sure I saw something out there."

I tell Mei about the monster and what it looked like, trailing through the water, with those orbs of pink eyes and silver-orange scales all magical and mysterious-feeling in the misty morning. I even tell her about how I think the monster looked at me, with purpose, not coincidence. How we looked at each other before she dove away into the water. It felt otherworldly; I tell Mei that, too.

When I've told her everything there is to tell, she just keeps on nodding thoughtfully, staring in concentration at nothing in particular, and says, "I believe you. You know? You're talking like I probably won't, but I do."

Normally, conversations like this would be funny. Like the way Rafael and I were talking about Lost Lake's conspiracies this morning on the bus. Around here, it's fun to joke about stuff like this; legends and cryptids and mysterious creatures are not all that off limits. But I'm not joking around, really, even though I don't feel super serious either. Seeing that lake monster just felt real. And talking about it with Mei made it seem even more like a strange part of our reality rather than some story made up for tourists. She makes me feel real. Like a fact instead of a legend.

My phone buzzes again and it shatters whatever serene headspace I've let myself get lured into. I grab it from the bed and see the most recent message. A text from Rafael.

Can you ask Mei if Jian is going to the fire tonight :D ;D

"Rafael is asking about your brother."

"My *word*. Why? Why does he have to harass Jian like that?"

I debate divulging my theory that Rafael is absolutely head over heels for Jian but ultimately decide to quietly see how that one plays out. Enough realizations for today.

There's a message from Dad reminding me that he'll be done with work around two in the morning, and another text from Joseph that I don't open. Just seeing his name on my phone makes me feel all weird and queasy. I really hope we don't run into him tonight.

The floor beneath us creaks as Mei stands up, holds out her hand, and hauls me up. When I'm standing, she doesn't let go. We just stand there, in the middle of my very small room, holding opposite hands and staring at each other.

"You're my favorite person," Mei says.

"And you are mine."

Look. The wi-fi is kind of spotty around here, but I've had enough panicked nights of Google searches to know what "asexual" means. I mean, maybe not completely.

Like right now. Mei is holding my hand and I definitely want her to keep doing that. And if she—*hypothetically*—kissed me right now, I don't think it would bother me. But beyond that, I don't really know.

When I dated Joseph, it was because he asked me out. When someone asks you out for the first time, you feel a little obligated to say yes. But Joseph always cared about things I didn't care about. Like making out whenever we were alone and touching my waist and my legs and— honestly, I just don't want to think about it.

I guess what I'm saying is, I'm standing here, staring at Mei. She's got a very sweet look on her face that is honest in a way I don't see with most people. Her cheeks are round and her lips are bright red and her bangs are kind of messed up from a day's worth of living. And I like her. I like her in a different way than I like Rafael and Jian, which is to say that I like her differently than I like my friends. Not more or less. Just differently.

And I don't know what that means. And I don't know if I will ever be able to explain that to anyone, even her, and that breaks my heart a little, but we've got this right now. Standing across from each other, holding hands, watching.

She has to leave to get ready for the bonfire. We're going to meet each other there.

Until then, I'll think about everything I just blurted out—about girls and kissing and monsters in lakes—and about the things I know about Camila Flores.

❧ 6 ❧

I GO TO A PARTY

IT'S NOT SUPER LATE when Rafael knocks on my door, ready to head over to the inlet fire, but bunches of dark clouds have started to gather in the sky, so it's darker than it usually would be. When I step outside, he hands me a bouquet of weeds and asks, "Will you go to the fire with me?"

"That makes it sound like we're walking to hell together."

He runs a hand through his slicked back hair, winks at me, and says, "I can roll with that."

I laugh and Rafael smiles really big because he can't hide the fact that being funny is, like, one of his main points of pride. But his face drops when we hear the rumble of tires on dirt and gravel and then see clouds of dust puffing up around Lake View as a shiny Toyota screeches out of the park.

"I swear I'm gonna kill that fuckin' guy," he mutters.

Mr. Jones is out in front of his trailer, sitting on one of

the creaking porch steps with a cigarette, and he yells, "Language, Vega!"

"*Sí, sí!*" Rafael waves him off and glares down the road.

"Was that Kyle?" I ask, walking behind our trailer to try and get a glimpse of the car again—I didn't recognize it. "Did he do something?" That's kind of a dumb thing to ask. With Kyle, the question isn't *Did he do something*; the question is, *What the hell did he do?*

"Yeah, it's fucking Kyle." Rafael kicks at the ground and stones spray across the scraggly grass in our yard. "My mom and I were watching one of those house shows, you know?"

"You watch HGTV?"

"Fuck yeah I do. Except we're watching it, and then fucking Kyle comes home, piss-ass wasted and fucking yelling about how my mom's never happy to see him, doesn't give a shit about him. Starts calling her all this nasty shit, you know? And my mom whispers to me, like, leave if you're gonna do something stupid. Like she thinks I'm gonna throw hands with this guy—and I wanted to— but I'm not gonna leave her alone in the house. It was just a whole afternoon of that, until Ma had to leave for work. The fucking dick-ass shithead."

"Rafael!" Mr. Jones yells.

"I know! *Lo siento*, jeez."

For the record, I definitely agree that Kyle is a dick-ass shithead. But I don't say that in front of Mr. Jones (we're still trying to borrow his boat tomorrow) and I don't say it in front of Rafael because he seems kind of wound up right now, punching the air and kicking things as we start the walk over to the inlet.

I watch over the water as we walk beside it, trying to catch a glimpse of that monster, listening to Rafael ramble until his words eventually tumble over to Jian.

"You gotta help me here, Callie. I don't want him to hate me or anything."

I'm not totally sure how we got here, conversationally. I'm still a little stuck on Kyle and on Rafael living in the same house as him. But I try to play catch up. I tell Rafael, "I don't think Jian hates you." Which is probably technically true, but not hating someone isn't exactly setting the bar high for how they actually feel.

"Okay but how do I... Shit. I don't know how to talk to him."

I try to be as casual as I can when I ask, "Why do you want to?"

"What!" Rafael skips ahead and turns around so he's walking backwards, waving his arms at me. "Are you kidding me? He's, like, the coolest person I know—"

"*Jian Huang* is the coolest person you know?"

"Yeah! He's, like, really smart. But not in the school way, you know. In the common-sense way."

And it's really sweet. Rafael is smiling—the small kind of smile. I say, "Ah."

"Not everyone is like that."

"Guess not."

"Plus, he's pretty hot."

I almost trip over a tree root at that, but Rafael hardly notices; he's so lost in his head about all this.

"Look," I say, trying to sound practical. "You don't need to be so nervous around him, Raf. Don't try so hard to get him to like you. You're cool. He probably already does."

"Ha." Rafael falls back into step with me, his shoulder bumping against mine every few steps. "I don't know about that."

We have to walk in this long arc along the edge of the lake to get to where the fire is. Branches snap under our feet and rocks scatter when the toes of our shoes hit them. Spring is definitely here—all of the usually-scraggly brush is tangled with new vines and dark leaves. Moisture gets trapped in the trees and bushes and everything smells like wet dirt. It also kind of smells like rain, which I'm not a fan of. But if it does start to storm a bit, I guess that would mean the bonfire is off, which wouldn't be too bad.

Walking to the inlet means taking a stroll where the houses get more expensive as you go along. On the way to the fire, we can see all the different tax brackets that exist in Lost Lake. A fun, economic journey. Raf and I come from square one.

"I really hope he shows up," Rafael says. It sounds like he's talking to himself and I'm just around to hear it. I do hope Jian shows up, though.

"When have you guys ever hung out?"

"I'm his Spanish tutor!"

"You never help me with Spanish!"

"*Estudias más duro.*"

"What?"

"You're welcome."

He laughs and pulls me against him with an arm around my shoulder. And this is it. This is Rafael, you know? Joking and sweet and kind of a little shit sometimes and it's awesome. There isn't much light out at this point, but his face still looks bright. It's not like he was just a few minutes ago, talking about Kyle. It's like the farther away we physically get from all that, the lighter he seems.

It's nice.

Until it isn't. Until his face clouds over again and at first I don't realize why, but then I hear it.

We're at the part of the lake where things start to get really nice. I mean like private-docks and four-story-houses nice. And we're down a bit on the bank, ducking under piers as they come along, skittering along the edges of the water in the warm lights from giant houses. But only one of those houses is really commanding our attention.

It's the yelling. Coming from an open window on an old A-frame. Rafael noticed it first, but now that I've heard it, I can't focus on much else. It sounds like a man and a woman. I mean, you can hear the man—you can definitely hear him. And there's something to the sound of the two of them. Something in the edges of their voices.

It's dangerous and dark and unruly, and the woman sounds scared. She does. I'm walking past her house, her life, and I can't deny that one feeling. She's scared. I can hear it—I can *feel* it.

Rafael is shaking his head and exhaling through barely-parted lips. Around my shoulders, his arm is tense.

We duck under their dock—it's an older one than the others, and it reaches farther out into the water.

"Do you think—"

"I don't know, Callie."

I'm not sure what that answer means, but I'm not sure what I was going to ask either. I don't know how the two of us can tell something bad is happening in this house without even really hearing the words that are being said.

A louder phrase. From the man. And then silence.

"Rafael."

He doesn't say anything.

Crying. There's crying. Faint, but I can hear it.

We keep walking, shoes brushing through rocky dirt, coming out from under the dock and heading for the next one. What are we supposed to do? It's like we're walking away from danger. But you can't escape a situation you were never a part of. Whatever was happening in that house is still happening. Just not to us.

I look back at the house. The lights from the window look inviting. From a distance, everything looks fine. The dock stretches out, unassuming over the blackness of Lost Lake. And we move on.

Rafael tugs at my hair, which I'm sure is a tangled mess at this point, since I have done nothing along the lines of styling. He says quietly, "You look nice, C."

"Thanks."

And then it's over. The traces of panic and outrage spilling out of the yelling house. It's gone, I guess. For us, it's gone.

As far as looking nice goes, I definitely do not, and that becomes especially evident once we actually arrive at the bonfire. There are more people here than I expected. Some just starting to dance, others joking around by the firepit, talking with giant, animated arcs of their arms.

Everyone looks so comfortable and excited to be here. That might have to do with the alcohol; I can already smell it on the air, mingling with the campfire smoke, but it still makes me feel a bit out of place. How are parties like this easy for people? I don't get it.

Even though Rafael is one of the few guys around here who really put any kind of effort onto his appearance, he looks like the Puerto Rican James Dean, hair all slicked back, fancy leather jacket. All of the girls look incredible —all sundresses and crop tops and perfectly applied makeup. Only around here could I show up to a bonfire feeling underdressed.

The bonfire is set up in a giant fire pit in the middle of the inlet. It's a little lake-beach kind of thing, only instead of sand, we have clay mud with loose stones scattered all around a little clearing and surrounded by trees. Beyond the fire, Lost Lake stretches out, long and wild, a vast dark void beyond the warm lights of the party. I can see Lake View on the other side, and it looks tiny and insignificant beneath the wide, tree-covered mountains above it. Someone strung lights between the tree branches over the clearing, and a few people are perched on lawn chairs or sitting on old blankets. A lot of them are holding plastic cups and the whole area smells like cheap alcohol.

I look around for Mei but can't find her. The whole setup is pretty nice, but there are a ton of people from school, which is still weird and intimidating. Realistically, they all probably know who I am, but I still feel like a complete outsider here. I've hardly been to any of these inlet parties and I'm not really sure how to jump into the whole atmosphere of it now. It's like I'm taking a test I didn't make time to study for.

Some of Rafael's gang are around us in a second. Instantly, it's loud jokes and friendly pushing and wild laughter. They all look like they belong to a 1950s biker gang, which I'm guessing was coordinated. I sometimes forget that Rafael has his own group of people that I'm not a part of. He's different around them than he is with me. More himself, less himself, I don't know. Just different. It's all Rafael. More Rafael than I ever see when we're talking about Kyle. I'm glad he looks himself again, but I feel a little bit like an intruder among them all, like I didn't put in the time to qualify for their antics.

The smell of the campfire is just hitting me when I feel my phone buzz in my back pocket. Another stupid text. And it might be from Mei or from my dad, but I'm kind of scared that it's from Joseph, so I don't even check the message.

Rafael and his little gang start to wander away to get drinks and I feel weird about following them, so I don't, which just makes me a little bit mad. I don't even know who I'm mad at. No one really, just generally. Because now I'm like a free agent, socially, and I didn't sign up for that. And I don't mean angry-mad; I mean stressed-out-and-kind-of-scared mad, because now I'm wandering repetitively around a party I didn't even want to come to, constantly pretending to look like I'm on my way somewhere. To some group or conversation or red-cup cocktail. It's a dumb situation. I could just sit by the fire or walk around by the trees, pretending that it doesn't bother me to be around a bunch of people from school while we're *not at school*. I like everyone here well enough; I'm just realizing now that I don't really know anyone like this. Like in a casual, we've-hung-out-outside-of-English class way.

I try to settle in somewhere, but I can't make myself sit still anywhere for more than thirty seconds. I can't clump onto the side of a conversation I wasn't invited to. I'm working myself up, I know I am, but I can't stop moving and switching and walking around with no actual destination in mind. Honestly, I think that if I tried to talk to anyone, I might start crying, which is ridiculous. I'm being ridiculous.

I look out across the lake and I can see the long dock where the couple was fighting, and beyond that, the twinkling lights of Lake View. I feel drawn towards them in a visceral way. Maybe I should just walk home.

"Hey there, trailer trash."

It's the last thing I want to hear, and from the last person I want to hear it from, but for some reason, when I see Joseph heading my way, a little part of me feels thankful. Here is another person. Here is someone to engage with. The opportunity to interact with someone feels nostalgic at this point, even if it all might turn sour soon.

"Why don't you answer my fucking texts anymore, Catwell?" The momentary spell of relief fades quickly with his intense tone, but I still can't bring myself to walk away from Joseph. Whatever is between us is familiar. This—him and I—it's something I know. I'm getting drunk on familiarity and it feels riskier than alcohol.

"I haven't been near my phone much," I tell him. He

meets me where I'm standing by the edge of the trees. The faraway firelight casts shadows shaped like coffins over his deep-set eyes. I don't like that we're in semidarkness together. The string lights over here have flickered out. There's party chatter all around and some music pouring out of a speaker, but it's like the darkness muffles all that sound.

"Okay." He smirks.

I hate how blatantly not on the same page we are, as always. He wants this, I want that. I'm uncomfortable, but I don't really think Joseph cares. Maybe that's harsh, though. Maybe he would care if he could tell what I'm feeling. Maybe I'm not sending the right signals. But I don't know how to point out my discomfort. I feel like I'm being obvious about not being interested. I also kind of feel the total opposite of that. I haven't outright told him I don't want to talk. I haven't blocked his number, you know? If Joseph is still around, I must be putting out some vibe.

He's leaning towards me and I get this sick feeling in my gut. I think about when we were together and how I got that same feeling. Trapped, stuck, heart beating way, way too fast.

Joseph is close now; I can smell his cologne and it just kind of ruins my thoughts until the only word I can comprehend is a loud and vicious *No!*

I don't say it out loud. His lips brush against mine and I'm afraid. Because what if I say it? What if I say "no" and nothing happens?

I don't like thinking shitty things about people. I don't like thinking that people might be bad. But I think you can tell. If you're with someone who respects you, you can tell, and if you're with someone who does not...

There are just some gut feelings I don't want to prove right. And I'm frozen. He steps closer to me and I can't really back away—there's a tree behind me and I feel rough bark pressing into my hands, closer than I realized. I kind of turn my head to the side and Joseph's nose bumps into my cheek. I can feel him taking in a breath to say something. I realize his arm is braced by my head, against the tree. I realize that even though a lot of people are around, we're still in the dark and everything is fuzzy, and Joseph and I are separate in a way that I hate.

Joseph starts, "What are you—"

And then he stops. Because in the clearing, by the edge of the water, there's this huge splashing noise, followed by choruses of drunken, '*What*'s and '*Dude, did you see that?*'s.

Joseph turns toward the commotion and I slip away from him then, walking—maybe running—to the water's edge. The monster. I swear it had to be the monster. Just like how this morning, just when things were getting bad, she showed up. And it's such a relief to have a reason to get away from whatever was happening with Joseph.

When I get to the water, I'm dizzy. I try to look for something out there—some flash of a tail, or sign of ripples—but it's just dark, endless water and houses lighting up the forest's edge.

I'm not really sure what just happened. I'm out of breath from running or worrying or something. I look around for Joseph because I know that's who I was just with, but I don't see him anywhere and after a second more of glancing around, I don't try to find him.

He tried to kiss me.

He *did* kiss me.

And I didn't say a damn thing.

Nothing makes any sense; my mouth doesn't feel like my own. I grab a cup from a plastic table at the opposite end of the woods, just to have something in my hands for a while, and I wander. I'm not sure where; I'm not sure if I even actually move.

I know I'm staring at the water. Perfect and clear, like glass, reflecting smoke and clouds and nighttime. I watch and listen to see if I can figure out what everyone else just witnessed. At first, I think someone must have jumped into the lake—a bold move, considering the water is still probably less than 40 degrees—but that's not it. After a few minutes of eavesdropping, it seems like no one can tell what caused the splash. A drunkenly thrown rock? Some over-zealous fish? It was too dark to tell. Too dark to know.

I wish I hadn't come here. I wish I knew if Joseph could see me right now. I wish I could go back to this morning and stare at the Lake for hours, never having to take my eyes off it. I wish I could find that monster. I wish I could get away.

7

THE TIPSY DANCER

"THERE YOU ARE!"

When I hear Mei's voice, it's like my brain and my body come back together. I can feel my toes for the first time in what feels like a millennium. There's some tension in my shoulders that I didn't realize was there, and I feel some of it fizzle away into the smoky air.

I turn around and there she is. Mei Huang, wearing this maroon romper I've never seen before. The middle is made of flowery lace. She's got her hair up in two buns, sprinkled with silvery glitter, and when we see each other, I can feel that our expressions are the same. Huge smiles. Relieved smiles.

"Finally!" Mei says.

"Finally."

She's surrounded by some girls from the dance team who all look lovely and who all wrap me in wobbly, alcohol-fueled hugs.

Camila is with them. Cool Camila. She doesn't seem drunk. She seems sure of herself, a confident little half-smile on her lips, giant curls cascading halfway down her back from a high ponytail. She's aesthetically hard to look away from. I don't get crushes much (just the one) and I don't really ever feel attracted to people because of the way they look. But with Camila, I think I can kind of begin to understand what that's like. She holds herself in a way that catches your eye. She isn't someone you want to miss.

And it hits me that I've never really seen her like this before—out with a big group of people. Camila isn't the type who has a lot of friends; at least, I don't think she is. I never thought about it before, but the only person I really remember ever seeing Camila with is a French-Canadian girl that transferred to our district the same year Camila did. Émilie, I think her name is. I wonder where she is now.

Mei smiles at me over the shoulder of a girl who's still got her arms wrapped tightly around my own and is squealing, "Callie, ohmigod you look so, so cute!"

When I tell her the same, the girl clutches her chest and says, "That is the sweetest thing I've ever heard, thank you!" before kissing my cheek and running to follow the already retreating group of dancers.

But Mei and Camila hang back with me.

"Hey guys," I say. And even though it didn't bother me a few minutes ago, I suddenly feel like I should have put more effort into my outfit or hair or something. I am a mortal among goddesses. Dramatic, I know, but that's what this feels like.

Camila nods with that little smile still caught on her lips, "What's up, Catwell?"

It's weird hearing my last name in Camila's voice. It feels familiar, like we've talked before about more than just dispersion theory and interval scales, which we have not. For some reason, I feel a little proud.

She says, "I'm gonna grab a drink. See you around? Maybe we can dance later?" She smiles at Mei, who nods vigorously and watches intently as Camila touches her shoulder briefly and walks away.

I try not to let it bother me. That this could be a thing, Camila and Mei. Mei and Camila. But I'm starting to understand the 'you can do better than him' comment from Rafael and Mei. When it comes to anything possibly happening between Mei and I, she could do better than the nervous trailer park girl who thinks there's a monster in her backyard. Mei deserves someone legendary. I'm pretty sure that isn't me.

Instead of going for the question I'm actually curious about (something along the lines of *What the hell is going on?!*), I ask Mei, "Hair glitter?" And she laughs, a little louder than what makes sense, which means she's at least a bit tipsy.

"I like it," she slurs. Maybe tipsy is putting it lightly?

"Oh, believe me, so do I." I scoop an arm around her waist and tug her arm around my shoulders and she leans into me, a comforting, warm weight against my side.

And I didn't know I felt like crying again until I'm standing at the edge of Lost Lake, with Mei beside me, wobbling on alcohol-induced Bambi legs, and I feel all my would-be tears dissolve. They bop excellently around in the air, shimmering in the campfire smoke and string lights. I breathe. Even with all this Camila stuff, even when I'm a little bit afraid of what's going on, it's just like this with Mei. Calm and easy and honest.

Another breath. "She's really pretty," I say. Because it's the truth. And because maybe it would make Mei happy to be with Camila. Maybe she just needs to know that it would be okay.

But she says back, "You're really pretty!" And it's not even funny how fast my face heats up. It's like I'm right next to the fire, even though we're standing several yards away from it.

Behind us, people are cheering and laughing, getting rowdier as the night goes on. The water in front of us is smooth as glass, annoyingly undisturbed.

"You looking for your monster?" Mei nudges my shoulder with her head, which makes us stumble sideways a bit.

"Yeah. I guess."

Mei sighs, loud and dramatic. "I hope you find it." She rolls up and down on the balls of her feet. "You all good, Callie Cat?"

"All good." Not a lie. Right now, I'm pretty much fine. I mean, I'm a little afraid to go back to where the real crowd is. I don't want to see Joseph again; I don't know what I'd do.

"Okay, okay, okay," Mei says. She takes the cup from my hand—I don't even know what's in it, I kind of forgot I was holding it—and downs it in one go.

"Damn."

"Let's dance!"

For the record, I love dancing. I used to take actual classes at Mei's studio before money got a bit tight, and she still sneaks me into some of her lessons when possible, but even this kind of thing—remixed pop songs and jumping up and down against a bunch of partial acquaintances—is kind of awesome. At least, it is with Mei. I think anything would be awesome with her.

Jeez. Why am I so sappy?

I throw the empty cup into a trash bag slumped on the ground, and Mei is dragging me out to the little dirt patch of a dance floor, and something by Katy Perry is playing. I'm smiling and we're dancing, and I get lost in it all.

For several songs, that's my life. Dancing and jumping and laughing with Mei. The fire makes everything orange and bright, and everything is warm and I'm out of breath, but in the good way. Because Mei is across from me, I'm holding her hands, and we're spinning around and jumping. It's hot and magic and wild. It's a moment that I cannot stop existing in. I can't let it go.

I'm not sure how many songs go by or how many minutes have passed when I finally have to stop and breathe and go get something to drink. But when I get back to the patch-of-dirt dance floor, Camila is there, twirling Mei in perfect, ballerina spins.

I won't let it bother me.

I can't let it bother me.

But then they're kissing.

My heart stops. *I* stop dancing, smiling, moving, breathing. I stop and it's all I can see. Camila and Mei. Mei and Camila. Rafael swoops in beside me. I feel his leather jacket press against my arm, and I look up and he's talking to me. The party comes back. The dancing people and the fading fire and the music. It all feels lesser than before. Faded. Cold. Camila is nowhere that I can see. Mei is stumbling towards us on wobbly legs. I feel like I just lost something. A part of my life. I can't remember how I got to this point.

A crush. I have a crush—maybe more than that—on my best friend. And she came here to dance with someone else.

Everything comes back into focus with the sound of Raf's voice. "What?" I ask.

"I said, is Mei gonna need a ride home?" Rafael nods his head her way. "Seems kinda wasted."

"Uh." I try to remember if she drove here. "Yeah, maybe. I think one of the dance girls brought her. I'll call Jian." I have to fish Mei's phone out of her pocket to get his number, which is absolutely ridiculous, but I let him know where we are, and he says he'll be here right away.

Rafael waits by me after that. People are still hanging around, but the crowd is starting to thin. I bring Mei to a blanket by the fire and sit next to her. She's completely delirious, which is weird.

"I've never seen her drink so much," I tell Rafael.

He shrugs. "Finals stress?"

That's possible, but still not like her. If Mei is stressed about school, she talks about school. A lot. Getting drunk on cheap vodka? That's not really how she operates.

Rafael, for his part, is cautious and steady and intently watching us both. I ask him, "Did you not drink?"

"Nah." He stares at the fire and settles in next to me. "Didn't want to mess around with that tonight."

I'm about to ask him what he means, but Rafael is

talking before I can manage to. He says, "Were you with DeLarino?"

And of course he saw—of course he did. Hearing him ask about Joseph makes my lungs do funny things. This isn't something I want to talk about.

"Yeah."

"Dude." He takes his eyes away from the fire and looks at me. "What the hell?"

"What the hell, nothing. We were just hanging out." And kissing. Ugh.

"Okay." It sounds more like "*If you say so,*" a tiding of caution. Rafael turns back to the fire and the flames are dying down, but they still cast shifty orange light across his face. "He's bad news, Callie. I don't get why you mess around with him."

"Who cares, Raf? It's whatever."

He doesn't say anything. He just shakes his head and I can tell he's holding back words, but I'm pretty sure I wouldn't want to hear them. Whatever goes on between me and Joseph is between me and Joseph. I never understood why Rafael was so uneasy about us dating, and I don't understand why he's giving me crap for it now.

I know to be careful. I know to be cautious.

There are just the sounds of crackling fire and drunken laughter and Mei's sleepy breathing between us until Jian calls. He's a little more frantic than I remember, asking where the hell we are and if everyone is okay. When Rafael realizes who I'm talking to, his eyes go all wide and he gets very still. His whole thing with Jian must be more intense than I even realized.

I think it's tense between Rafael and I, but as we haul

Mei to her feet, whatever unspoken thing was going on between us evaporates. A few minutes later, Jian is waving to us from his car, parked on the edge of the woods. His expression when he sees the three of us—a drunk Mei bracketed by Rafael and me—would be funny under any other circumstances. But I can feel the panic radiating from him, and I immediately want to take it away.

"Oh my God, oh my God, oh my God." He grabs fistfuls of dark hair with both his hands as we get closer to him.

"No," Rafael says. "Just me."

Jian ignores him and leans down to squint at Mei's face. He even tries to take her pulse.

Rafael laughs, but it's soft, "Oh, come on, she's *alive*."

"She won't be for long." Jian straightens up and looks at me and I'm hit in the face with all of his worrying. His eyes are screwed up in strangled dread. "Mom is going to kill her."

Rafael starts walking towards Jian's car, so I stumble along after him with Mei mumbling vaguely between us. "It'll be okay, Jian," Rafael says. "We'll help you figure it out."

"Yeah," I try. Watching Rafael out of the corner of my eye, he's calm. I can be calm too. "She can stay over at my place."

"Yeah." Jian shakes his head and looks between Rafael and me before hurrying to pull open the car door. "Yeah, okay. Okay."

The four of us pile into his car, Mei and I together in the back. She leans against my shoulder and grabs my hand, and I'm pretty sure she's literally about to vomit, but I still can't stop a small part of me from feeling all fuzzy and stupid inside.

I don't catch much of what's being said up front. Rafael is talking quietly, and Jian is nodding along. Whatever he's saying must be calming Jian down. His shoulders fall at least an inch by the time we make it out onto the main road.

Into my shoulder, Mei mumbles. "I'm a mess." Her eyes are closed, and she might just be talking in her sleep, so I squeeze her hand and try to hold her still around the curves in the road.

Jian seems to have relaxed a bit, but he's still got his eye in the rearview watching us about fifty-one percent of the time. It's like he's trying to make sure we don't fall out, until Rafael grabs his shoulder and says, "Stop being so jumpy, man, it's just alcohol."

The clock on the dash reads 12:21. Dad won't be home, which I'm thinking I should be grateful for. Most people my age, coming home from a party smelling like a mini-bar, would be relieved to know that their parents won't be around for another two hours. But not being able to see my dad right away kind of makes me panic, and I think I would pull out my phone and text Terry from work if Mei weren't spilled across my lap, trapping my phone in my pocket and holding my hand in hers.

"She needs to throw up," is the first thing Rafael says when we get back to my place.

"What?" Jian. Horrified.

"Come on, man, she'll be wrecked tomorrow. She needs to get it out of her system."

I hear Jian mutter, "How would you know?" and I

silently hope Rafael doesn't respond to that in a snarky way. I don't think he will. I think tonight, maybe, the two of them are getting somewhere.

I can't spend too much time worrying about what either of them said, though. Before I'm even through the front door, Mei has shut herself in the bathroom. It's bad. We can all hear her from the yard. I wince in the doorframe.

Jian drops his head down low and rubs at his eyes. "What the hell was she thinking?"

And although he's been on edge since the moment he showed up, I hear the weariness in his voice, and it hits me in the center of my chest. Because this isn't something Mei does. She doesn't get drunk, and she doesn't get sick after nights of crazy parties.

I shift a bit from our little wooden steps and they creak happily under my feet. Rafael looks solemnly at Jian and leans against the car, right next to him, without saying a word.

When I head back inside, Jian is muttering quietly to Raf. I try not to eavesdrop. Inside, though, from the living room, I can see Mei leaning against the bathroom door, looking at me funny as I pull the front door shut.

"Callie?"

"Yeah?"

"I think I drank too much."

"Yeah."

"I think I'm still maybe tipsy."

"The tipsy dancer."

"Oh shit." Mei squeezes her eyes together like she's

suddenly got a headache. "Dance. Tomorrow. I have classes to teach."

"Ha."

"Ugh!" She rolls back into the bathroom and I hear the shower cut on, so I set a towel out for her on the sink and check back outside. Jian and Rafael have both made their way back into the car. They're sitting next to each other and having what looks like an actual conversation. When Jian notices me, he nods his head a couple times and flashes a half-smile. I duck back into my room and wait for Mei.

We were just in here, getting ready for the fire, talking about Camila and prom and how she asked Mei to go with her. Everything that happened tonight feels like an escalation of that. It feels too much like cause and effect. Maybe I want it to feel like that, though. Maybe I'm making up a version of all of this that makes the most sense for me. Selfish.

I want so badly to know what she's thinking. And she's got to be going crazy with all this thinking. Is she trying to figure out her sexuality? That kind of thing is insane. And this is all happening to her so suddenly. I debate asking her right now through the shower curtain in the next room if she's okay. She can't be. Not totally. Too much is going on.

When I go to check my phone, I see the battery is dead —it never lasts long anymore—so I plug it in and crawl into bed. I want to hear from my dad. I debate waiting up for him, but I feel so tired. I try to stay alert enough to hear when Mei cuts off the water, but my eyes are drooping almost right away. Physically, I didn't even do anything crazy today, but once I'm under the covers, it's like my body is convinced I was playing intense games of contact sports all day. I try not to think about why. I try not to think about Joseph, or Rafael being hurt, or my dad's half eaten piece of toast, or Mei kissing a girl I didn't even know she was friends with.

I've never been good at thinking, or maybe I'm too good at it. I don't focus on one thing, I focus on, like, nine. And half of them are totally pointless and the other half are utterly stressful so sometimes, even when I'm beyond exhausted, I can't fall asleep.

But then I think of the monster. How she was gliding through the water this morning. Maybe even splashing around at the inlet. And it's sort of relaxing and maybe that's crazy, but whatever. I think I'm crazy most of the time so I might as well be crazy about something fantastical.

I'm on the edge of dreaming when I feel the mattress dip down next to me. For a split second I'm freaked out until I see that it's Mei, groggily collapsing beside me. I scoot over to make room and she nestles into the comforter, and I'm definitely awake now, but that's okay.

I try to be glad that Mei is beside me and ignore the fact that I might lose her. I know that's selfish. To think I could lose someone. It's not like Mei *belonged* to me or something. But she's been in my life. She's been in my favorite parts of it. All the times I thought, *If this is love, love is easy.*

I'm sappy. I'm over it.

I do love Mei and I'd admit that to anyone, but this can't be about what I feel. If Mei thinks she might be into girls, I'll help her figure it all out. I'll be with her until it all makes sense and forever, as long as she needs me. I only know two things about Camila, but I guess I'll have to learn more. Because if Mei really does like her, I want to find the ways that I can like her too.

I'm not losing Mei. I guess it just feels like I *could* lose a part of our relationship I didn't even realize was important to me. Realizing how much I took for granted between us makes my stomach hurt.

On my pillow, lighting up under strands of Mei's freshly washed hair, my phone buzzes. I reach over her to check the screen. It's a message from Joseph.

Had fun tonight.

Mei kissed Camila. Joseph kissed me.

Another message from Joseph comes through. *Text me tomorrow.* I roll onto my side. I think, maybe, I might.

8

LEATHER JACKET

WHEN I WAKE UP, silvery-bright light pours into my room through the small window by the ceiling. It's cloudy outside—I can tell.

Yesterday was nice, but it's been threatening to rain for a while now and today might be the day the clouds finally break. Mei is still passed out beside me. Well, kind of beside, kind of on top. Her left leg is flailed awkwardly across both of my knees and my arm is wedged between a pillow and her face.

Twin beds. I try not to laugh. We used to sleep like this without a problem. We grew, I guess. We got taller but honestly not by much; Mei's barely 5'1 and I hardly stand any higher. I didn't realize it was happening, the growing and the changing. We've known each other for so long and we grew in a lot of the same ways. That kind of stuff is hard to notice as it's happening.

Mei is snoring. I try not to think it's cute. I try to focus on literally anything else instead.

The monster. The monster living in the lake behind

my house. It's been a whole day since I saw her. I can't see what time it is, but I don't hear the sounds of anyone shuffling around outside, and we've kind of got a close-proximity living situation set up here at Lake View.

I awkwardly pick my way out of the bed and then faceplant onto the floor, making too much noise for this early in the morning and causing my shelf of DVDs to rattle together. Mei turns away from the noise but doesn't wake up. I grab a blanket and my phone and run outside before I can make any more early-morning noise.

Of course no one is awake. It's Saturday and I don't think the sun's even breached the mountains. Not that I'd be able to tell— it's even cloudier out here than I thought. Still sort of cold but already muggy and humid. The puffs of fog coming off of Lost Lake are denser than they were yesterday.

Jian's car is still parked in the gravel behind our trailer. He's asleep in the front seat, not even reclining back, just slumped on the window, his face all squished against the glass. I've never seen him like this—all vulnerable and unguarded. I think about how last night I didn't even have his phone number, and how that's kind of weird considering I've known Jian for six years.

Across his chest, someone's draped a leather jacket. Rafael is nowhere to be seen.

I pull the blanket tighter around my shoulders. It's one of those scratchy, crocheted ones. I think my mom had it growing up. It feels like the sort of thing that's lived multiple lives. Kind of how it felt looking into those rose-pink eyes yesterday. Like looking into the past, like living with something that existed long before you.

Or maybe just staring at a fish.

As I make my way down the cracked cement launch point, I pretty much convince myself I made this all up. I've got to be going wild. It doesn't feel like I am. But pink eyes? Does anything in nature actually have pink eyes?

The lake is glassy and grimy-green as ever. Looking at the surface—totally undisturbed, reflecting what I'm sure are storm clouds up above—it's difficult to reconcile the two versions of Lost Lake that are in my head. Version one produces a constant and inescapable green sludge and occasionally contains deceased trout; version two, living (breathing?) magic. It's like seeing a dream in real life. It's not supposed to happen. The monster is hard to believe but impossible to deny. An anomaly. Maybe those conspiracy theorists were right.

I scroll through my notifications. There's a text from my dad from two in the morning letting me know he's heading home. Then one from Rafael, sent twenty minutes ago, around five a.m.

I'm gonna be the one to stand you up today. An entire row of sad faced emojis. *Can't make it out on the lake but Jones said you could use his boat. The old-ass green one, with the edges falling off.*

I glance over at the row of boats and spot it immediately among the long grass. "Old-ass" definitely checks out, but it's a boat, which is kind of thrilling. I've lived here my whole life and never actually been out on the lake. I run through the weekend in my head, trying to figure out when I'll have time to go out on the lake and look for the monster. I'm squinting across the water like maybe that'll make something appear.

My phone buzzes again. More emojis. A string of different types of tiny, colorful boats. I didn't realize there were so many.

Get that son of a bitch in the lake, Catwell.

Before I can read too much into why Rafael can't make it out this morning (he's tired from last night, right? Just tired), I hear gravel crunching behind me.

"Morning, sunshine," Mei yawns. She's carrying a cup of coffee and wearing an old Harley Davidson sweatshirt she must have left here at some point. She raises the mug, "Your dad sent this."

"He's awake?" My impulse is to ask a couple million questions. Was he eating? Did he look tired? Out of it?

But Mei answers the most important ones before I have a chance to even ask them. "He was making eggs and, uh, had a cup of orange juice, I think?"

That's a good sign. Making breakfast is a good sign. That's not always something that's easy to do.

Mei takes a sip from the mug before passing it to me and shimmying under the blanket, so we're huddled together, hiding from the little early-morning chill. I was almost about to go inside, make sure those eggs actually get eaten, but I feel a little steadier about everything with Mei next to me. She knows about my dad's eating disorder. Or at least, she kind of knows what I know, which feels like it isn't a ton. But right now, for a little bit at least, that's enough.

"You feeling okay?" I ask her. Less than twelve hours

ago, she was vomiting in my bathroom, something I've absolutely never seen her do.

I feel her nod against my shoulder. "Last night was…"

"Weird?"

Mei lifts her head up and looks at me, and we both laugh. "Weird. So weird! Oh my word, I'm so sorry."

She leans her head against my shoulder again and we both kind of keep laughing. It's a relief, I guess, to know that we're kind of on the same page. I'm not worried about nothing. She got crazy-drunk. Mei isn't a crazy-drunk person. She's a three-sips-of-someone-else's-drink person.

"So." I nudge her shoulder. "What happened?"

"Ughhh!" She buries her face in the corner of the blanket and when she moves it away from her face, it's only enough for me to see her eyes. Dark brown with smudgy eyeliner. She drops her hand completely and looks back out at the lake. "I was just so stressed about this Camila thing!"

Ah. My stomach bottoms out at Camila's name, but I glance at Mei so that she'll go on.

"She was just there, at the fire, being really sweet, hanging out with all my friends…"

"Kissing you."

"Kissing me. Yeah."

I feel really stupid all of a sudden. Of course Mei would kiss Camila. She was hanging out with Mei's friends. I don't do that. They're all really nice. I'd love to hang out with them. I just get nervous or something stupid like that. But that's what you do when you're friends with someone, right? You put yourself out there to understand their world.

I actually might be the shittiest person I know.

"Am I overreacting?" Mei says quietly after a while. She's still got her eyes set on the lake, like she's trying to spot whatever monster I think I saw out there. "Like, am I overthinking this? If I like her, I should just go for it, right?"

I have to clear my throat before I respond. I don't want to sound like I'm about to cry (am I really about to cry?). "Do you? Like her?"

"I don't... *not* like her."

"Hm." It's shitty, but it's all I can manage. I'm the worst.

Mei is still watching the lake. Or maybe she's just thinking, and the lake is only what happens to be in front of her. And what am I supposed to do? Confess my love to her? I don't even know what that means. I don't think I even realized I was crushing so hard until right now. But I think about Camila, and how she gets along with Mei's friends already. I've known Mei for six years and I still feel weird talking to the dance girls. And then there's the fact of Camila kissing Mei. Maybe it would be easy with them; maybe it would be a good thing for them to be together.

She's got the right corner of her bottom lip between her teeth. Lost. And I realize that none of that matters. Not really, not right now. "You're stressed about this."

Half a laugh. "Yeah."

I squeeze her a little tighter against me. "You're not overreacting. It's a lot. It's new. But... you'll figure it out. Seriously." I look out at the lake. What can I even do to make this all easier for her? Feelings and kissing and relationships—this stuff is confusing. It's crazy and wild and there's no method to figuring it out. But Mei will. I know she will. And I will support her and hold her up until she does.

Mei nudges her head into the crook of my neck and rests there, and for a second, we're just in this little warm pocket of *us*. Of Mei and Callie. Eventually, she asks, "Did you see that monster again?" I'm kind of surprised she brought it up.

"Uh. No." I think about that splashing at the party last night. Maybe that was the monster. Or maybe it was just an excitable fish. "I don't know. I might have been hallucinating the whole thing."

"I want to look for it with you," she says. "I want to see it. Ah, shit—" Mei pulls her phone out from her hoodie pocket. It's buzzing but stops suddenly. "Nine missed calls from Mom. My word."

"Ha."

"Ha. Callie, you have no idea. What the hell am I supposed to tell her?"

"We fell asleep listening to Johnny Cash CDs."

Mei starts to head back and because we're wrapped in the same blanket burrito, I stumble along with her. "That's good. She'd like that."

Back at the trailer, Jian is shuffling out of the car, stretching and glancing around like he forgot where the hell he fell asleep. The leather jacket falls into the dusty gravel and he realizes it for the first time.

"Jesus, Mei," he says when he notices us. "What was all that?"

I think by *that* he means *last night* and I think that by the hunched forward set of Mei's shoulders, she doesn't want to talk about it.

"Cool jacket," I say. Jian looks at me with wide eyes, like I just caught him in the most criminal of undertakings, and looks down to the coat.

"It's, uh. Could you..." He runs a hand through his hair and as Mei slides into the passenger seat of the car, she mouths *thank you*. "It's Rafael's. Would you..."

"Yeah. I'll give it to him."

"Thanks." Jian ducks into the car then back out again. He's really way too tall to be related to Mei. "Thanks. For letting us crash and returning the, uh—the jacket. Yeah. The jacket."

"The jacket."

Jian nods and climbs into his seat. I look at the jacket and at him and at Mei, slouched down in the passenger's seat, looking like she could fall asleep again in a second. I really cannot believe last night. The more I think about it, the more alarming it all seems. Mei getting so drunk is not something any of us are used to. There may be nothing in the lake beyond, but there is certainly a weird kind of magic at play in this rocky excuse for a driveway. A million things are about to begin. Or maybe just a million hours of sleep that need to be caught up on.

Jian pulls away and in the cloud of dust he leaves behind, I text Rafael to let him know I'm coming by to drop off his jacket. I'm only now letting myself wonder again why he had to bail this morning on the boat, and suddenly it's all I can think about.

Where was Kyle last night? I can't remember. I'm

genuinely hoping that I'm being paranoid right now, but all of it fits too naturally together. Rafael wouldn't want to be drunk if he knew Kyle was going to be around. But he got home late last night. He wouldn't tell me if he got hurt.

I try to remember if I saw Kyle's car around when we got back to Lake View. I don't know. All I know right now is that I have to get to Raf's.

As I pass our trailer, I peek through the screen door to see what's going on in the kitchen. Dad's still at the stove, humming a bit. That's good. Humming is good.

As I make my way across the park, I don't see Kyle's car anywhere. He could have left. He still could have been here last night and left early this morning. He still could have done something. He still could have hurt someone.

There's someone shuffling around in Rafael's place when I get there and knock on the door, leather jacket clutched in my free hand.

"Rafi?"

I hear Jaslena—Rafael's mom— call, "Callie, is that you?"

"Yeah, I have Rafael's jacket."

"Rafael!" She yells something in Spanish down the hallway and then, "Unlock the front door!"

Then I can faintly make out Rafael's voice, muttering in Spanish, all blearily like he's hardly even awake. When Rafael finally does come to the door, he's wearing his red Adidas hoodie and tying that green bandana on. Under his eyes, the skin is gray and ashy. At the door, he's blinking too much, like it's difficult to keep his eyes open. His fingers keep slipping on the knot of his bandana; he can't quite get it in place. "Aye, Catwell. Did you get my text?"

I hold up the jacket as he clicks open the lock and leans against the door frame. "Jian wanted me to give this to you."

Rafael straightens up and, holding onto the door-frame, he leans outside and swings back and forth in front of me like he's scanning all of Lake View for Jian.

"Is he—what did he say?"

"Uh." I squint at Raf. "'Could you give this to Rafael?' He seemed weird. Did you do something to him? What did you do?"

"Aye, nothing!" Rafael steps outside and finally gets his lime-green monstrosity tied right around his head. "Jeez, Callie, grilling me first thing in the morning."

I shove the jacket at him and smirk a little. "Some-one's jumpy."

"You wanna know what happened?" He lowers his voice and steps farther outside; the old wooden stairs give a bit beneath the full weight of the two of us. "We talked for, like, hours, and then…"

"What?" I'm smiling, but Rafael is looking at me with wide brown eyes and I'm realizing I genuinely have no idea what he's going to say next. Did they fight? Are they upset about something?

"He kissed me."

My stomach drops. "What?" It's all I can manage. I'm surprised. Why am I surprised?

"Jian Huang." Rafael is smiling now, eyes all bright and lit up. "Kissed my face. And he did it on purpose."

I blink. Is everyone just kissing everyone else now? I

have literally no stakes in the Rafael-Jian situation, but it still makes me feel kind of stupid. *Jian* kissing someone? I didn't even know Jian cared. About anything. Let alone kissing Rafael.

People kiss. People like kissing. And I get that. I mean, not for myself I don't, but I've seen movies. I've seen the way this kind of thing changes people. Makes them happy and excited. But sometimes I just forget that it happens in real life. Sometimes I forget that other people think about it, about kissing and more than kissing actually happening in real life. Sometimes I forget, and I feel pretty stupid when that happens.

"Was it—" I start. I don't even know what I want to ask. My world is spinning. I hate that I feel blindsided by this. "What then? You just, uh, you left then?"

Whatever that means, it was the wrong thing to say. It's like I blew out whatever fire was burning behind Rafael's eyes. "Well, yeah. I was already past curfew, you know? I didn't want to leave, but..." He's fiddling with the zipper on his sweatshirt and all my worries from the walk over here come flooding back to me. I want to ask if Kyle was here when Rafael got back, but I'm also worried that's out of line.

"Listen," Rafael says. "Don't, like, spread this around? I don't want word getting back to." He nods his head back to the trailer door.

"Your mom?"

"No. Uh. Just. If Kyle finds out somehow. He'll just be shitty."

"Right." I remember us talking last night at the fire. Before we came back with Mei. Were we fighting? I don't want to fight with Rafael. I should leave this alone; I should trust him. Shouldn't say anything. I should— "Are you okay?"

Rafael bats a hand at the air and goes, "Psh," like it's not a big deal. And my eyes snag on his shoulder where his hoodie slipped a bit and he tugs it back in place too quickly. It wasn't enough time to know or to see, but I swear there were bruises there. New ones. And I open my mouth. I start to say something, but before I can—

"I'm okay, Callie," Rafael says. There's a little bit of an edge to his voice. A warning. "Seriously."

I should say something more. Or do something more. But I don't know what action to take. I just kind of nod and it feels like the wrong thing to do, but it's what gets Rafael to stop looking at me like we're about to have a yelling match. And that would be the worst, wouldn't it? Nothing would be worse than that.

"We'll take the boat out some other time, then?" I say.

"Yeah. Yeah. That sounds good."

We stand there for a second, staring at the things around us instead of looking at each other. My eyes catch on the leather jacket Rafael is shifting from hand to hand, and I think about how he really looked good in it. It's a good style for him.

My God, I can't believe anything that happened last night.

"So," I say. "You're telling me *Jian* was the one to kiss *you*?"

"Callie Catwell, I swear on my fucking life!" Rafael says. His eyes are wild and happy again. All of the tension between us dissipates for now and it's just me and Rafael.

I didn't even realize he was holding himself weirdly until he wasn't, until he became comfortable again. It makes something in my heart calm down. "Jian went in for it before I even realized it was happening."

"My God."

He's laughing now, loud and bright and it reminds me of looking at the lake. I know that two different realities exist within it—monster, no monster—but it's impossible to believe the one while I'm looking at the other.

Happy Rafael.

Hurt Rafael.

Both true. Both impossible.

I pull him in for a hug, which I think takes him by surprise. He goes really still for a second before wrapping his arms back around me. He says, "Thanks." And I'm not sure what it means, but I hug him a little tighter. When I pull away, Rafael is smiling, and I think I am too. And he tells me, "You know I'm gay, right?"

And I throw my head back laughing and hug him one more time. "I know."

❀ 9 ❀
TIMING

Breakfast is magic.

My dad is sitting down as I walk in. On the stovetop, one of our frying pans is pushed back away from the burner, scrambled eggs still sizzling. Dad smiles at me and it's not a tired expression or a hard one to believe. He looks happy. Relaxed.

I take a deep breath.

I don't want to jinx anything, but this morning feels miles away from yesterday and in the right direction. Dad just seems so at ease. It's difficult to keep my smile from looking too obnoxious.

I sit down with my coffee and a plate of eggs, just like Dad, who has a decent serving in front of him. He looks up from his plate and says, "You're very popular this morning."

"I don't know." I sip the coffee—it's completely cold at this point. I really don't care. "I think the Huangs were just here to see you."

"Ah. And Rafael?"

I can feel myself wince just a bit at the thought of how not-himself Rafael is whenever we're talking about Kyle. I should say something. About the bruises, about Kyle in general. At least to my dad, right? Or would that make it worse? I don't know. I just don't know. I can't stop thinking about the bruises on his shoulder. They looked mean. They looked hateful. But that's all in my head. Maybe it is, I hardly saw anything. I roll my own shoulders back. "Him too. He's your biggest fan."

And then my dad is telling me about work. Real enthusiastic. Says it's going really well. I'm not going to lie; that makes me feel one thousand times better. Even though he might just be saying good things for my sake.

"They're working on a report right now," he says. "On a new plant species they found in the woods here. Interesting stuff."

"Are these the kinds of plants that, like, eat animals and/or people?"

"I wouldn't know. I'm just a secretary," Dad says. Then he takes a smug bite of eggs. Actually *smug*. This is a good day. I swear it's going to be a good one.

My brain is a mess of worrying about a million things while being excited for a million others. When little things go the right way—when my dad doesn't have trouble eating breakfast— it's too easy to let the bad stuff go. The bruises and yesterday's toast and all the attention from Joseph (three more texts since I've been inside). It's easy to grab onto the stuff that's all right and ignore the rest, just totally shut it out.

Some days are bad days? Bullshit. Some days are awesome.

I tell him, "Dad, you need to abuse your power more. You've got, like, insane access. Even if you made something up, people would have every reason to believe it was true."

"That's the spirit." On his plate, there's really only a bit of crust left, which is almost a whole piece of toast better than yesterday morning. "You heading to work?" he asks.

"In a bit, yeah." Even the promise of six hours at Joey's Sandwiches doesn't get me too down.

"I'll drop you off."

My dad and I have always gotten along. I think we never really had the room to fight. When my mom died, she took the space for that kind of stuff with her. Not that she was, like, an angry person. I just mean it kind of sucks not having a mom, so I can't take my dad for granted. I literally don't think I'm capable of it. I hate to admit it, but I think it means there's some stuff he and I don't talk about. Like the anorexia. Like my mom. We only have those conversations when we absolutely need to. It doesn't bother me. It doesn't *not* bother me, though.

But sometimes the days are good, and it feels like not talking about that kind of stuff is fine, maybe even for the best. We're making it work, my dad and me. We're fine.

Outside, the sky is looking darker and more ominous than it was even twenty minutes ago. It's going to storm later; I can feel it. I steal a glance at the lake as we're leaving to see if I can catch the monster in action. Nothing. Mr. Jones' boat is practically facilitating plant growth, but I feel a tug in my chest knowing that it's there. I have to get out on the water.

For now, I tug my Sandwich Expert hat on and slide into my dad's old pickup.

Lost Lake has a circle of shops and row homes that sort of make up the town's center. The dance studio is at the far end—Beetle's, it's called—and it's easily the coolest architectural situation around here. The old, warped glass windows stretch up from the top floor and curve over the front edge of the building. I'm not sure what the place was before Beetle's took over, but it's one of those old historical buildings the township likes to brag about, like the church across the little plaza, or the boarding school down the street. Beetle's is magnificent.

Beneath it is the crumbling brick monstrosity that is Joey's Sandwiches. My destination. Dad pulls to the curb out front and I can see the grimy paper menu we taped to the front windows tearing at the edges.

As I start to push the door open, my dad asks, "Will you be able to get a ride home?" His voice sounds higher than usual, so I pause, my hand on the door. Little raindrops are beginning to freckle the windshield.

It's just finding a ride home. That's nothing out of the ordinary. But Dad sounds... strange.

"Uh, sure. Why?"

"I don't want you to worry," he starts. And it's instantly worrying, of course. "I'm going to be working a few more hours at the labs than usual. I'm going in at twelve today—"

"Twelve?" I let the door go and sit fully back in my seat. "That's like, not even ten hours off. Is that—like, is that even legal?"

"Yes, Callie, it's—"

"Is that a good idea?"

In the car, Dad says, "I think so. I think the timing is good."

All I can think about is yesterday morning. In the kitchen, he couldn't even sit at the table; he couldn't even look at his food. It was like that, just yesterday.

"What about, like, eating at regular times? And not overworking yourself and—and everything they always tell you—"

"Callie, some days are going to be bad days. Right? The extra money will be good. This will be an adjustment, but I can make this work."

He's trying to sound rational. But we were just in the hospital. It was two years ago. It was yesterday.

There should be fewer bad days, I think. There should be fewer before he overworks himself into a hospital bed. I look over to Joey's; the lunch rush is in full swing and I cannot imagine myself going in there and dealing with customers after having this conversation.

"I have to go."

Dad sighs. "I'll be home pretty late, but tomorrow— I'm sorry, I shouldn't have waited to tell you. We'll talk about it tomorrow, okay?"

"Okay." Not okay, absolutely not okay.

I shuffle my way through the crowd of people in line at Joey's and shoulder into the back room. The manager grunts a greeting in my direction. The crowd is backed up to the door. In the kitchen, they're behind on orders. They're glad I'm here. It's good timing.

KNOWLEDGE IS COMFORT

WHEN THE SHOP CLOSES, it's full-on storming outside. I'm a little bit ridiculous when it comes to storms, as in I'm kind of afraid of them. Not like hiding-under-the-counter-rocking-back-and-forth afraid. Just the kind of afraid where I want to do all that but feel like it's—as previously stated—ridiculous.

I've hated storms since I can remember, and I couldn't really tell you a reason why. It's just a feeling. Too much noise, too much movement. Usually, closing the shop is the only part of work I don't mind. I'm alone. I can get work done. But with the thunder outside, it's just making me jumpy.

For a second, I wonder about the monster out in the lake, and if stuff like this bothers her. Storms. Lightning. Rain. I wonder if she even realizes it's happening. I try not to wonder about my dad. I can't right now. Except I have to. I have to know if he really is doing better. And if me leaving things like I did made things worse. It might have all been fine, the timing might have actually been good. I might have screwed up an okay plan.

I'm wiping down the counter and holding on way too tightly to the blue food service towel when this giant burst of thunder snaps, and my bones vibrate in response, I swear. I know it didn't shake the floors or, like, shatter the windows, but I'm imagining all that in my head and it's all very unpleasant. It feels like it lasts forever, like the booming will never stop.

Really. It's not stopping. There's this endless thumping echoing through the shop. What the hell?

I open my eyes, not even sure when I closed them, fully expecting to see some giant monster tornado outside, but then I scream.

And then I laugh (but keep screaming, for just a bit, in my mind).

Mei is standing in the front window, rain blasting down all around her, knocking her fist against the locked front door.

"My God."

"Let me in!" She's smiling and laughing, and I have no idea why.

I rush to unlock the door and before I can get out a, "What the hell are you doing out there!" she's got her arms around me and her whole body up against mine and I'm a chaotic mess of freaked out and incredibly happy.

Outside, the rain pounds against old pavement and stormy winds make tree branches rustle beneath the rolling sounds of thunder. We're a part of the chaos outside until a gust of wind slams the shop door shut.

Then everything is muffled and quiet and it's just me and Mei.

"Rain hug! I locked myself out of the studio! Please hang out with me!"

It's a lot. It's all a lot.

I get it. I'm all wet now and I'm supposed to pretend to be annoyed and we're supposed to joke about it, but honestly, with Mei right beside me, right against me... I don't know. It's making my head clear.

I focus on the most normal thing that I can. "You locked yourself out?"

She pulls away from me, pushes rain-soaked bangs away from her forehead. The Harley-Davidson sweatshirt from this morning is tied around her waist and all she's got on is her leotard and some nude tights. In her left hand are her ballet slippers.

"And you're not wearing shoes."

"I locked myself out, remember?" She nods. "After waiting outside with one of my preschool students. And these shoes were expensive." She shakes them in my face and I laugh. "I'll walk barefoot on a million sidewalks before I let anyone's dance shoes get water damage."

I finish up the cleaning with less effort than is totally professional and I use my key to let us in upstairs. The dance studio has its own entrance outside which leads immediately to a stairwell covered in the handprints of all the students that practice there. Mine is at the bottom, bright purple, right next to Mei's. But the less sentimental route is through the back of Joey's, up some stairs that creak way too ominously and are supposed to be lit by bulbs that burnt out many months ago.

"This staircase is haunted for sure," I say, like I say every time we find ourselves scrambling upwards through the dark to the studio this way.

"Oh my God, I know, I know, hurry." Mei is laughing and grabs me around the waist as she passes by. By the time we get to the studio door, we're both kind of cracking up and out of breath. Mei leans against the push bar and heaves a breath, smiling at me before collapsing into the studio.

As cool as Beetle's looks on the outside from the street, the inside is even more amazing. The rain is streaming down the already warped glass and I feel like I'm in some kind of perfect bubble of existence where the storm doesn't bother me. Nothing does.

Mei pushes some barres out of the center of the floor and fiddles around with the speaker system in the corner. She asks, "Are you busy? Do you have anywhere to be?"

I laugh. "You know me." And for clarification: "No."

"Samesies." A song comes on, sudden and loud, through the speakers. "Wanna see my audition choreography?" she yells over the music. I nod and settle in against the mirror, the giant windows backlighting Mei as she makes her way to the center of the studio.

She's talking about college auditions, which is crazy. We're only juniors. I mean, I know a ton of people are thinking about that stuff already, college stuff. I know a lot of people are preparing to apply, like Mei. Maybe like Camila. I've never given college much thought, which up until now has been a normal-ish thing. Or at least, an acceptable one. Junior year is when college is supposed to be important. But I don't want to think about it. Because college is money, and money is the reason my dad is pushing his limits.

"Okay, okay, this is where I start..." Mei is watching herself intently in the mirror behind me, bobbing her head on each beat until she starts to move.

And then I'm not thinking about anything anymore. Not college or Dad working more hours or all of those texts from Joseph. The rain is washing over the glass around us, and I'm thinking about Mei. Just her. Just us. Just here. And it's beautiful.

I watch the shapes Mei's legs and arms create in the air as she moves. I think it used to bother Mei that she was bigger than the other girls at the studio. Maybe it still does. I hope not.

Because she's strong in the intimidating and breathtaking way that forests and oceans are, and I don't know how to explain it. It's like, there were always mountains and there were always gusts of wind and rushing waterfalls. There is an art to the world that is older than anyone who has ever lived in it, and when you watch Mei dance, you can see that old and constant magic.

Maybe I'm being dramatic. Maybe I'm not.

It's a modern dance routine that Mei is doing. All heavy limbs and swinging movements. Mei hasn't decided which schools she's applying to yet. She's furiously researching all kinds of options, though. She wants to double major in dance performance and biology, which sounds intense and impossible but so, so right for her.

Mei jumps up and crashes back to the ground just as a spike of lightning shoots across the sky. It all makes my heart jump.

The song ends, the dance stops, and Mei smiles. She's breathless. I clap and say, "Are you kidding me?!"

"What?"

"That was incredible!"

"You liked it?"

"Yes!"

Mei laughs and leans forward, letting her arms hang down until they touch the floor. "I'm so tired." She slumps down next to me against the giant mirrors and looks up at the giant windows. As she watches the storm cascade around us, I watch her, just for a second. And we're perfectly still. Just breathing. Just existing.

"Wanna hang out here for a bit?" she asks. "I can give you a ride home."

"Lovely."

And in about .2 seconds, we're huddled together on the dance studio floor, watching videos on her phone and mindlessly waiting out the storm. Mei reaches across the wooden floor and snatches at her backpack. I am, in the back of my mind, aware that I have homework or studying to do, but I'll probably spend the next few hours with my statistics textbook open, doodling in the margins of a homework sheet.

When Mei opens her laptop, there already a million tabs open, which is pretty standard for her. "I've been doing some research." Of course she has. She's always researching something. For school or dance or personal curiosity.

There are too many tabs open right now to see any website names, but the top of her screen just looks like a miniature banner of pride flags.

"So, like, gay research."

"Correct."

With Mei, knowledge is comfort. When it comes to academics or passions, or literally anything relevant to her life, she looks into it. I mean crazy looks into it. Memorize-the-Wikipedia-page-and-exhaust-all-known-YouTube-videos-on-the-topic kind of looking into it. As far as coping mechanisms go, it's a pretty useful one. And even though I know this is exactly what Mei does, I'm caught off guard. She researches. She works to understand. I just never expected her to try and understand *this*, of all things. We've never talked about sexuality before, and now I'm realizing for the first time that I kind of wish we had. It feels weird that we haven't, I guess. Like this giant, unprocessed part of myself is now here and hulking all of a sudden, even though I didn't realize how big it was.

I'm asexual.

I've known that for a while, but I've never talked about it. And right now, that's making it all feel very unreal. I'm thinking maybe I *don't* know things. At least not about this. There are a million little tabs shining bright at me that make me think I don't understand asexuality at all. I couldn't possibly.

I definitely have a crush on Mei. Can you have crushes and be asexual? Sure. Yes. I've read about this. But I probably could have read more, right? What even is a crush?

I'm sort of in full-on internal panic when Mei says, "I'm being crazy." And I look at her because that's ridiculous. We can't both be the crazy one. But when we look at each other, we get that. Neither of us is crazy. When we're with each other, we're not crazy; we're us. Mei and Callie. Callie and Mei.

"You're not," I laugh. Laughing is such a relief, and I suddenly feel it all over again. That strange enraptured calmness I felt when I saw the monster in Lost Lake. Calm doesn't sound right, though. It's more like *real*. I feel very much a part of the world right now.

"I just want to know what's going on, you know?" She's clicking aimlessly through the tabs, glancing over each page for a few seconds before moving on. "I just mean, I don't want to mess around with this. With Camila. She's nice, you know? I don't want to just—" Mei waves both of her hands around in front of us and I don't know why, but I get it. She's being careful. Cautious.

"And honestly, Callie," she adds, "I thought I knew about this stuff, but I really don't."

The giant mirror makes everything in here so bright. The rain-filtered light is so serene, and I know she's confused and worried, but in here, Mei just looks so much like herself. Everything is really clear. I mean, it's super unclear I guess, but the way she's researching and hunting for an answer, that's very much *Mei* and it's very hard to look away from. It hits me that trying to figure this stuff out—sexuality and who to date and just all of it—is very wild and very brave. I think you can't help but be yourself, but it takes some kind of courage to try and understand what being yourself even means.

She's clicking through the pages still and when she opens one with *About Asexuality* scrawled across the top in giant purple serif font, my heart squeezes.

"I just feel really naive."

I look at Mei. "You're not naive."

"I am a little naive."

"About this, maybe." I lean into her arm until she looks at me with frowning eyes. "But most people are."

"Callie."

"I just mean, don't be hard on yourself." I sit up. "This isn't easy. For anyone. Even Mei Huang."

She drops her eyes to where her hands are resting on the keyboard and dips her head until she's resting on my shoulder. "It feels like it's easy for other people. I know it's not, but it kind of feels like it is. Reading all of this—"

"You're at the beginning. The people writing this stuff —they've been figuring it out for years."

"I want to have been figuring it out for years." She shifts her elbow back until her hand is slotted in mine.

"I know." I stare at our hands and the way we fit together and the wildness of it. Of us.

Mei says, "I want it to be easy." She looks up at me and she laughs. I want it to be easy too. "You really would kiss a girl?"

My phone clatters from my free hand—I'd forgotten it was even there. "Uh."

Mei scrambles to sit up and when her hand leaves mine, I *feel* it. "I just mean, you said—when we were at your place yesterday..."

"Right, right, yeah." My phone clatters against the floorboards as I fail to pick it up for the third time in a row. Above us, lightning flashes and then, seconds later, a clap of thunder shakes all the bones in my body. I should tell her. I mean, I *could* tell her. I could tell Mei right now that I'm asexual. I could tell her that I like her. Seriously like her.

I won't. Probably I won't. But the possibility of it is thrilling.

I glance at her computer screen again and she's on Twitter or something and there's a chat box up and before I look away, I catch Camila's name. And it kills me. But this is Mei. This is my best friend. When I said I saw a lake monster in my backyard, she didn't even look at me funny, you know? I have to support her. I'm going to, no matter what. Even if that means watching her fall in love with someone who isn't me. I mean, obviously! If she's happy, if there's a chance something could make her happy, I'm not going to stand in the way of it. Or *her*.

"I don't know." I shake my head and try to smile. "I don't know why I said that."

I can't bring myself to look her way. When my phone vibrates on the floor, I grab for it a little too quickly. I can feel Mei's eyes on me as I open up a message from Joseph. If she sees who it's from, she doesn't say anything.

You wanna hang?

It sort of makes me wince internally, but I can see the chat conversation Mei is having with Camila out of the corner of my eye. I can't come out to her right now. I can't tell her that if there's anyone worth kissing, it's her. Only her. And for a second, I just feel really, incredibly shitty about everything.

Maybe it's self-pitying or pessimistic or some guilt-complex at work, but I feel awful. Joseph wants to hang out? Sure. Whatever. An awful time for an awful person.

I text him back, *Sure. Pick me up at Beetle's?*

And he almost instantly replies. *Be there in a few.*

Mei sighs and I still can't make myself look her way. I'm scared to see what she's saying with her face and her eyes. With her voice, she says, "I wish I just knew everything. Like for sure, knew it all."

"Me too," I tell her. "Me too."

DIFFICULT

I'VE BEEN in Joseph's car for about thirty seconds and already want to jump out the window.

He says, "You're so tense all the time, Callie. You need to relax." It makes me laugh but only because that's one of the most ridiculous things I've ever heard. Have you ever been with someone and it is immediately obvious how you are nowhere near on the same page? How they don't understand a thing about you, and it's probably because they aren't trying to?

To Joseph, I'm not a thing to understand. I think to him, I'm just a thing.

This is ridiculous.

I am ridiculous.

I almost ask Joseph to take me home, but honestly, I know my dad isn't there and I don't want him to get the wrong idea. Besides, what else would I do? Worry about my dad for eight hours, or until I lull myself to sleep with some movie I've seen twenty times? It's better to be out.

To be social. To try not to think about Mei chatting with Camila.

Be supportive. Be supportive. Be supportive.

And be normal. Normal people would be into Joseph. Normal people would be glad he's taking an interest. He's the attractive one that works out and always smells like fancy cologne. I'm lucky.

We're going to his friend's place—one of the people who put on the bonfire last night—which means there will probably be a bunch of guys playing video games in a decked-out and darkened basement.

I'm basically spot on. I forgot about the energy drinks and marijuana, though. What an afternoon. There are various *Catwell!*'s and other very bro-ish greetings. One of the guys says, "Aye, Joey brought his girl!" And I hate the sound of that so much that I almost bolt before I even sit down.

I don't really focus on any of the conversations. They're loud and mostly about things that I don't care about. I'm shoved between the arm of an old sofa and Joseph, who keeps glancing at me and trying to get me to engage, and I start to feel bad that I'm not trying harder. I'm just staring at my phone, waiting for my dad to reply to the last two texts I sent him.

And I'm trying to not let this moment make me uneasy. I'm trying to get over Joseph and the way he puts his arm around me or rests his hand on my knee. I'm trying not to let it bother me. I'm trying to understand that people *like* this. People like to be close to guys like Joseph, even when they don't know a thing about him. Even when he doesn't know a thing about them.

I wish, I genuinely wish, that I didn't feel so uncomfortable right now. But I do. And I don't want to say anything or brush his hand away. Cause then I'm *being bitchy, Callie. Just chill.*

When we were dating, he said that all the time. I never mentioned it to Mei, or Raf.

"Yo," he says to me quietly. But it's the kind of quiet that this room full of guys smirks at and tries to listen in on. "You want to get out of here?"

"Uh." I want to *leave*. I definitely don't want to *get out of here*. I know what *getting out of here* means. I could easily just walk home. It doesn't sound like the rain is too bad anymore. But I don't want Joseph to think it's an invitation to follow me. And I really don't want to get into his car again. I don't want to be with him all night.

I'll try to be chill. I'll try to hang out with people that aren't Mei. But right now, my teeth are so clenched together I'm afraid they might break. I'm somehow shaking and all tensed up at the same time, and I don't know what to say because Joseph is looking at me with those shadowy eyes and I can feel everyone else in the room waiting to see what I'll tell him. They're waiting to see if I'll smile and laugh and say, "Yeah, let's go." Or ignore him completely and give them a reason to talk about me for the rest of the night. I realize I'm just sitting here with my mouth hanging open and Joseph running his hand up and down my arm. Is that supposed to be comforting? What's the opposite of comforted? Right now, it's me.

My phone buzzes in my hands and the screen lights up, bright and glaring in the dark basement.

Dad.

"Hey!" I answer and stand up immediately. Joseph's hand falls from my arm, and it's like I haven't been able to breath for an hour and now there's suddenly air in my lungs. God, I'm being dramatic, but it's the truth. I leave out the side door with a little pointing gesture to the phone. If Dad said anything, I didn't hear it. My ears are buzzing. I'm going to walk home.

"Callie?"

"Yeah, I'm here."

"Everything all right?"

"Yeah." I don't look behind to see if anyone is watching me leave. I'm power walking along the lake's edge. I must look ridiculous. "Lost the signal, I think. What's up? How are you doing?"

"Good." He says it right away. "Are you okay? I've got a bunch of missed texts from you."

Oh. "Uh. Yeah. No, I'm fine. I was just checking in."

Silence. Then, "Callie—"

"No, seriously." There are little raindrops falling around me. It's not quite dark yet but the sun is setting behind storm clouds so it's impossible to see too far into the forest. "I was just, I don't know... bored. Just bored."

"Are you at home?"

"Yes." Right now, I'm picking my way through last night's party. There are a few aluminum cans laying around, and the string lights are still up but not lit. It's discomforting.

"Is there anyone you could hang out with for a while, instead of being alone right now?"

I almost laugh. "Um."

He can't be the one worrying right now. He can't be. We were only at home together for breakfast and he left for work before eating lunch. Being at work screws up the routine, I know it does. I know I've texted him a lot, but I can't stop thinking about all this. About how he isn't giving himself enough time to feel better. He isn't giving himself a fair shot.

Almost home. I'm almost home. I see little pinpricks of light from Lake View through the leaves. The rain is making noise, gently falling against the water and the trees, and I am too, stomping across wet gravel and dirt, but I swear I hear footsteps behind me.

If Joseph followed me here, I don't know what I'll do.

"Callie, I know this is difficult for you—"

"It's not difficult for me!" It's difficult for *him*.

I can't tell if I'm hearing myself walking or someone else. I speed up a bit. The fading floodlights of the park are a stupid kind of beacon. I spot Mr. Jones's rowboat in the long grass before I even see home. And that's my solution. If Joseph is following me, if Dad doesn't want me to be alone, I'll just go out on the water. Not that I'll be less alone out there. It just kind of feels like I won't be. It sounds stupid, but if that lake monster is out there right now, I want to be around her. I need to feel real again, I need to feel grounded. Everything is in the air, buzzing around me. I can't quite catch myself.

"Did you eat dinner yet?" I didn't see if he packed anything. Terry told me they got lunch at the cafeteria, but I think that closes at night.

"Callie... Yeah. I'm all good here."

That wasn't an answer and I don't believe what he's saying anyway. I guess I don't have a reason to think he's lying. But I don't really have a reason to believe he's telling the truth.

"Are you sure?" I ask him.

"I'm—yes, Callie, I'm sure." He sighs on his end of the phone and that slows me down for a second. Weary. That's what we are. I take a deep breath. He asks me, "Are you okay?"

No. But I feel better than I did five seconds ago I guess, which isn't nothing. "Yeah. All good here."

"Good." He coughs. "Good, good, good."

I'm coming up on the rowboat. I'm sure I made up the sound of footsteps behind me. And then I'm sure I didn't. The bottom of the rowboat is facing up and I run my fingers across it. There are scratches and dents that are rough and real beneath my fingertips, but it seems sturdy. I sit on the boat and say, "Dig up some conspiracy dirt, please. I want the street cred."

"I think you were onto something with the man-eating plant species," Dad says, all business. "Start that rumor, I think. See where it leads."

"I will. For sure, I will."

"Alright." I can hear shuffling on his end, and I try to take another deep breath. Okay. For now, in this moment, everything is okay. I'm still uneasy. I think I will be for a while. I don't think he ate dinner. Some days are bad days. Some days are bad days.

I wish there were fewer of them.

"Take it easy tonight, Callie. Get to sleep at a normal time?"

"I will." Probably not. I'll try, I guess. "Text me when you leave."

"Will do."

I almost ask about dinner again, but I think maybe I shouldn't. I think it's annoying or it stresses him out. I don't want him to worry about me. I just say, "I'll see you later."

"Love you, Callie."

"Love you, too."

When Dad hangs up, I don't feel great. I hear those phantom footsteps and every time I blink, I see bruises on Rafael's arms or Mei kissing Camila. I feel Joseph touching me and I kind of want to scream.

Why the hell do I put up with Joseph?

The second I think about it, I feel awful. I'm not *putting up with him*. If I wanted to stop talking to him I could. If I'm uncomfortable, that's on me. Maybe that's why it bugs me when Rafael talks about how Joseph is bad news, because it's not about Joseph. It's about me. If I really didn't like him, I would leave him. Me sticking around isn't Joseph's fault—it's mine.

I flip over the rowboat and look around to see if Mr. Jones is watching. Rafael said it was okay, but still. My reasons for going out now are stupid.

If Joseph does come over to see where I went, I don't want to be at home when he does. He can't get to me on the water. Even if he didn't show up, I don't feel like being alone in my room right now. I've got too much buzzing around in my brain.

Even though the night is just getting dark, just getting a little bit chilly, I'm going out onto Lost Lake. I'm going to look for a monster.

For some reason, I feel like the idea that she's out there is the only thing keeping me safe.

12

MOM

THE PROBLEM with being an internally dramatic person is that when you come to and realize that you were, in fact, being dramatic, it's a very anticlimactic sort of situation. Maybe kind of funny, too.

I'm sitting in the middle of a freaking lake and it's about to be the middle of the night, and I truly cannot believe myself sometimes. I didn't see the monster. I'm starting to wonder if I ever even saw her in the first place. Maybe it was just some sleep-deprived panic delusion. I don't know.

I do know that I'm cold, but I'm worried that if I go back home, I'll start being internally dramatic again. It's easy to not be dramatic in the middle of a lake at night. I'm in the midst of a dark void and I can see the glow of the town far away on the bank. Out here, though, nothing feels pressing or scary or worthy of concern.

Why didn't I bring a blanket?

I've honestly never been on the lake before. It's kind of beautiful. There are rows of lights along the edge of the water, blinking through the trees where houses are still awake and alive. I'm not too far out from Lake View, but it still looks kind of sweet from where I'm sitting. A glowing spot of light among the trees. There are too many clouds still hanging around for me to be able to make out any stars, but I can imagine they'd be nice.

It's quiet—so quiet—which is somewhere between peaceful and eerie. I'm pleasantly tired with it all, lulled into some kind of otherworldly trance. I almost jump when my phone starts buzzing. Another call. I kind of expect it to be from Joseph, yet it's Rafael's face that lights up my screen. I answer right away.

"Are you out on the lake right now?"

"Ha-ha." I say. And then, for clarification: "Yes."

"You crazy psycho." Rafael cackles and I squint towards Lake View until I spot his tiny silhouette at the water's edge. "You know it's twelve in the morning."

"I guess."

"She guesses."

"What are you doing?"

"I'm going to work!"

My word, I'm so worried about him. Maybe I shouldn't be. Martin's isn't the worst place in the world he could be right now. Still, it's not the best.

"Be safe."

"Yeah, all right. You too, you know. You're going to get hypothermia out there."

I laugh and he says goodnight and I'm so in love with him. I know that sounds dramatic, but I swear, this time it's not. I love Rafael. I love that he's in my life. And sitting in the middle of a lake, black water all around me, black sky above, it's like he's the only thing I can focus on, the only thing I can really see.

Silhouette-Rafael saunters off towards the main road and I watch him until he disappears into darkness. I can't believe him. He's kind of amazing. He says I shouldn't worry about him and he says that he's fine, and I think maybe that's true. Maybe he is okay and maybe he can work with his own situation in a way that I can't understand. Just like he doesn't understand Joseph and I. Rafael and I could both just be worrying about each other over nothing. He doesn't get why I'm with Joseph and I don't get why he puts up with Kyle. Maybe we're both actually just fine.

Maybe I should be doing more, though. I freeze up every time I try and say something about Kyle to Dad. Maybe I could talk to Rafael's mom. Or a school counselor? That's dumb. What would a counselor do? What could they do? I'll have to look into it.

After talking to Rafael, I feel weird about not talking anymore. Now, I'm far too aware of the nighttime. I start to row back to Lake View, only half-heartedly trying to keep an eye out for the monster.

I'm pretty sure there are rules about this—rules that prohibit people from being on the lake after sunset in a boat, a boat that probably doesn't have an up-to-date license. Not that anyone really bothers to enforce the rules over here. I don't know what to do with myself when I get back on land, though. Is it really past midnight? Dad won't be home until two tonight.

I head back home, but it's weird in here. All lifeless and dark, even when I turn all the lights on. Our furniture is so old, there's no way it's not haunting us. I don't mind our house most of the time, but right now, it doesn't feel like a great place to be alone and awake in.

Whatever happened at the bonfire feels stupidly long ago. Everything didn't change that night, but it feels like it did. Everybody's kissing someone else. Whatever. I don't want to think about it. Not right now. It really does feel weird to be alone, but if nothing else, I'm glad I got out of a night with Joseph. I slip into leggings and an old sweatshirt and sit down on the little corner of my bed where it meets the wall. My mom's blanket is in a heap on the floor in front of my DVD's, like it's deciding what to watch.

Ugh. My mom.

I don't really talk to my dad about this. I don't really talk to anyone about this. I miss my mom. Sometimes I'm fine. Sometimes I don't think about it for a while. But other times, I don't know. I miss her. I miss her so much that it feels like a physical part of me is just gone, which doesn't make sense. I only knew her for a few months and those were the first months of my life, so I definitely don't remember them. But right now, I'm feeling it. I'm feeling that I miss her and for some reason it's killing me. I think I would have loved her so much. I think I should have had a chance to.

I'm not sure why I get like this sometimes. It's a comfortable thought as much as it is a sad one. I miss my mom, which means I have a mom to miss, you know? It still hurts, but I feel connected. To what, I'm not sure. Connected to her? To life in general? It doesn't really matter. It's terrible and nice, and right now, it's me.

I slide onto the floor and under the blanket; it's made up of so many colors, I'm not sure what the idea was. It's a chaotic rainbow. I'll never be able to ask about it, I guess.

I stare at the DVDs in front of me, organized by color, from red to orange to yellow to green to purple to black to white. They all blur stupidly together now because I'm crying, and I guess this is the kind of crying that I don't mind, even though I don't think I deserve to be able to do it.

In handfuls at a time, I pull all the movies off my shelf. The buddy comedies, and the westerns and the ones about zombies and vampires and all kinds of monsters; even the artsy movies with artsy kids (Mei's favorites). I let them crash onto the carpet, clattering against each other, and once they're all on the floor, I shuffle them around until there's just a chaos of plastic cases covering the orange-gray carpet in my room.

One by one, I put them all back on the shelf. I don't even look to see what I'm picking up. Whichever one I touch is the one that goes next.

Napoleon Dynamite.
Little Miss Sunshine.
Juno.
Dazed and Confused.
Ladybird.
10 Things I Hate About You.

I never organize my movies like this. All mixed together. Genres and colors and stories being smashed next to each other on the light-colored, fake IKEA wood.

But I don't care right now. I don't care about anything.

I put DVDs on the shelf in whatever order I pick them up. Same, different, opposite. It doesn't matter.

And I feel safe. Or maybe I feel the opposite of that. But I'm definitely feeling. I'm definitely here and real and alive, which is a relieving thing to be. And that monster? Right now, I'm sure it's out there. It has to be. I'm surrounded by a weird kind of magic that makes believing things easy. As the DVDs go back on the shelf, scraping gently against particle boards and dust, I'm willing to believe anyone about anything.

When I'm done, the movie shelf looks like my mom's blanket. I wonder how long I'll be able to keep it like that.

My cheeks are wet—like, soaking—and I dry them off with the back of my sleeve and then laugh for a second. And then I stop. Maybe laughing alone in your room is crazy. Like, going-out-on-a-lake-at-midnight-to-look-for-a-sea-monster crazy.

I wonder what my mom would think about everything that's happening around here. I wonder what she would think about what's happened to Dad. And I wonder if she would want me to do something about Rafael and the way he gets hurt. I wonder what she would say if I told her I saw a lake monster out back. I wonder if she'd believe me.

I wonder what she'd tell me to do about Mei. I wonder if I would want to talk to her about it all.

No, I know I'd want to talk to her. I want to talk to her now. I think in any universe, in any reality, in any plane of existence, I'd want to talk to my mom.

But I'm here in a world she left over sixteen years ago,

and I'm sitting in front of a shelf of DVDs, crying onto a sweatshirt in the middle of the night.

I need to get out more, I guess. I miss my mom. I really do. And I didn't even know her, really.

I don't want to check my phone, but I don't want to be alone right now. So I do.

One text from Mei: *Okay, Camila is really edgy, but like, super nice?? I think it's really cool.*

One from Joseph: *The hell, Catwell?*

None from Dad, or even from Terry.

I need to think clearly right now. I need to not make this about me. I tug the blanket tighter around my shoulders and try to breathe deeply.

To Mei, I type out, *If you like her, you should go for it. Seriously.* Hitting the send button sends a shock through my arms that makes me feel like I need to shake my hands out. I guess I did it. I'm doing it. I'm being supportive. And maybe I'll get used to it. Maybe, eventually, it won't be so bad.

I text Joseph, *Sorry! Family thing! Want to hang out tomorrow?* And it takes me a little longer to send it to him. My thumb hovers over the screen because honestly, hanging out with Joseph tomorrow isn't really something I want to commit to. I think about what Rafael would say. To just ignore the texts and the comments and cut him out.

But then I get a message back from Mei. Her name flashes at the top of my screen, followed by a bunch of tiny pink hearts. Hearts for Camila. I hit send to Joseph.

I send out a quick, *any updates?* to Terry and then shut off my phone completely.

I think right now, I need to get away from my crazy

DVDs and the nothingness that is being inside an empty mobile home with a probably empty lake outside.

Empty house, empty lake, empty girl.

I throw the blanket on my bed and grab whatever random change I can find lying around in my room. If my mom could see me now, she would probably advise against what I'm doing. Gas station, middle of the night. Whatever. Martin's All-Night Gas and Grub is open. It always is. That's its whole thing.

I guess I don't talk about missing my mom because, really, I don't have a right to. There are hundreds of people that knew her better than I ever will, and whatever sadness they feel about her passing takes precedence over mine. Feelings and emotions and things—they don't exist just for me. I have to be okay with the fact that other people—people like my dad—were more hurt by losing my mom than I will ever be.

And I have to be okay with Mei and Camila. Those feelings, Mei's feelings, don't belong to me.

I don't feel so real anymore. I don't feel much at all right now.

I need to get out. I look at the wild shelf of DVDs one more time before leaving. I take a mental picture of them like that and then I run out the door.

13

OUT OF COFFEE

WHEN I PUSH through the glass doors of Martin's All-Night Gas and Grub, making the little rusting bell above them chime, I'm completely out of breath from climbing the gravelly hill to get here. A small part of me is starting to regret leaving the house, which is maybe a good thing. It *is* past midnight, and this *is* a gas station in the middle of nowhere, but I want to see Raf, and that's enough to keep me walking across the grimy linoleum farther into the store.

Martin, the honorable namesake, is at the register, which means Rafael is somewhere in the back, so I head to the coffee station to wait out his grand return. The industrial coffee makers kind of obstruct the view of the register and even the front door. And I know for a fact there aren't any security cameras up around here. It's not like crimes are routinely committed at Martin's. It's just that in Lost Lake, if you hear that something illegal went down, the first place you assume it happened at is Martin's. So I don't love that one of my best friends works here in the middle of the night. But maybe I'm just being dramatic.

There's a scrawny white guy hanging out in the corner by a cooler of ice cream sandwiches. He takes a drink from a steel water bottle in a way that makes me think whatever's in there is at least a little bit alcoholic. He's looking at me. I panic-pour coffee into a Styrofoam cup except the pot is empty, which, I mean, makes sense, I guess. The guy laughs and I'm worried he'll try to say something to me, so I just go around the corner of the aisle before he has the chance.

Here's the thing: there's a decent chance he's harmless. But there is still a little bit of a chance he's not. Either way, it's creepy. And that's why I worry about Rafael here. Because sketchy stuff has happened at Martin's before; semi-aggressive shoplifters, drugged-out yelling matches.

Sometimes it's harmless, but it very easily couldn't be.

When I round the corner, I see Rafael wearing his uniform, which consists of his regular clothes plus a nametag that cuts the "L" off the end of his name. He's got a box of very brightly colored candy and when he sees me, he throws a packet of sour gummy worms at my head. "Catwell!"

"Vega!"

"Try to catch your giant fish with those."

I grab the candy off the floor and toss it back to Rafael, "Yeah, okay."

"What's up, girl?"

"You're out of coffee."

He pulls his phone out of his pocket and checks the time. "Yeah. That would make sense."

I laugh. I hear the drunk guy shuffling around, and then the sound of the store bell chimes. I tell my shoulders to relax.

"Oh! Hey, you gotta see this shit they got on channel eight!" Rafael shoves the box precariously on top of a rack of candy and dives for the front counter, grabbing a dingy-looking remote from behind the register.

"You finished with those boxes, Vega?" Martin doesn't look up from the clipboard of papers he's flipping through.

"I will, you gotta see this, man. Look, she's still on."

Raf gestures to the tube TV hanging from the ceiling and hits unmute. There's a black woman on-screen speaking earnestly to some unseen reporter. Her jet-black afro is streaked with bits of gray and she fiddles with the ends of her curls as she speaks. She can't be much older than my dad. She looks tired. Exhausted.

"—in Lost Lake, just the other night—"

"Who is this?" Martin asks, but Rafael just waves a hand at him, eyes glued to the screen.

"It was something like a fish. But bigger. And it didn't look much like a fish," the woman says. My heart speeds up. I glance at Raf. He glances back.

The reporter interrupts her. "A fish that didn't look like a fish?"

"I'm not explaining this right..."

Except she is! I know what she's saying. She saw the monster. My monster. She knows.

Or maybe I'm just projecting.

"It had pink eyes!" Okay. Not projecting. "Huge pink eyes and scales—like a fish—but it moved differently. Looked like all those drawings of sea monsters you see. But it was there in our lake, I swear!"

The woman has her arms crossed in front of her, but she's talking wildly. And I know what she's talking about. It's like I can feel what she's feeling. It's magic and strange and a little bit sad.

I didn't realize I was stressed out about this until right now. Until I'm listening to this woman I don't know, talking about a monster I swear I saw, and I am honestly so, so relieved. I'm not delusional. I saw it. This thing, this monster, is real!

"Drama!" Martin says in a sing-song way. "That is some drama right there."

My embarrassment is immediate.

"You think so?" Rafael says, arching an eyebrow.

"Yes, I think so! This happens every couple of months, some whack job monster-hunter trying to stir something up." Martin shakes his head, going back to his clipboard. "I don't get it."

I'm pretty much completely uncomfortable at this point, but Rafael smiles at me and raises his eyebrows at Martin. "I don't know, I think she's telling the truth. She saw something out there."

"Oh, I'm sure she did," Martin says. "She saw a tree branch or something bobbing around and her brain made it into a monster, because this is Lost Lake and that's the kind of touristy bullshit we hear every day."

It's not like I told Martin about what I thought I saw on the lake, but I do feel really stupid hearing him say that. I glance back to the TV; the woman is gone, but some reporter is talking about her in front of the Lake. I don't take in what he's saying. It must have been filmed earlier. On-screen, the sky is bright and sunny.

Maybe Martin is right, though. Maybe I made up what I saw out there on the lake. It felt so real at the time, but I don't know. Maybe I wanted it to be true. Maybe my brain made a monster.

"Boo!" Rafael leans across the counter and smacks the pen out of Martin's hand. "You're no fun, boss-man."

"How's that candy? On the shelves?"

"Getting there. We're out of coffee."

"We're out of coffee, he says. It's two in the morning, my God."

Rafael slings an arm around my shoulders and tugs me away from the counter and the TV and Martin. "Come on, I'll make some more. Decaf." And then we're tucked away behind the coffee station. As Rafael digs in the cupboard beneath the coffee maker, he says, "Martin's an ass."

"He's right, though," I say. Even though I don't want to say it. But I guess people can be crazy. I guess people can make this stuff up.

"He's right? Bull*shit*, Callie. Martin's a dumbass." Rafael wrestles with a cardboard box covered in packing tape, and I hope he's right. Not that Martin's a dumbass (although I don't know, all-night convenience stores? Risky business), but I hope there really is something out there. I hope that woman is right. I hope we both are.

"Did you see anything while you were out there?" Raf asks.

"Nah." I lean against the opposite wall while Rafael tears open a packet of coffee grounds and dumps them into a giant filter. "Maybe I was just seeing things the other day."

"Don't say that." Rafael hits a button that makes the coffee machine start beeping until he hits the button about nine more times. "I was thinking about it—your monster—and I think it makes sense. If there's a monster in a lake in this world, it'd come here. We got weird vibes in this town. You know?"

"Oh, I know."

"Listen." Rafael turns away from the coffeemaker and tries to casually maintain eye contact in a way that feels the opposite of casual. "I'm sorry I bailed this morning. It was just kinda weird at home."

I feel like I have to stand still. Like if I move too suddenly, I'll scare this conversation away. Rafael is never the one to bring up his home life. And he's trying to talk about it now. I think he's trying to talk about it.

"You mean—uh, did something happen with—" I don't even really want to say Kyle's name because I know it pisses Rafael off. It pisses me off too, I guess.

"Yeah," Rafael says quickly. "I mean, no. Kind of. It was just tense. And I didn't want to leave Ma alone, you know?"

I nod, because I know our situations are achingly different, but yeah, when you've got one parent and something bad happens, you don't want to be anywhere near alone. Because that means they will be, too. My dad takes care of me, he really does, but it's just the two of us. We have to take care of each other. It goes two ways.

My fingers are itching to send out another text to Terry. But I left my phone at home, and honestly, I'm more worried right now about whatever it was that made things tense at Raf's place.

Before I can ask, Rafael says, "I don't want to talk about it." And he's smiling and it's the absolute worst kind of smile because it looks like it could just as easily be a frown. And I get not wanting to talk about things, I really do, but when does that tactic become dangerous? When is it time to step in and talk anyway?

Not now, apparently.

Rafael's phone starts ringing, which means that *Jump Around* by House of Pain blares across the aisle we're in, and he hurries to shut it off and shove it back into his pocket.

"Who was that?" I cross my arms and lean back. We're friends. We'll always be friends. There will always be time for the bigger conversations later.

"Shit. No one, Callie, calm down."

"So, like, a crush or something? Hold on." A new thought, an old thought. A thought I don't want to forget. "Jian." This makes him blush. "What happened then? After last night?"

Rafael blows air through his teeth and fiddles with a pale pink sugar packet. "Ah, you know. Playing it cool." He readjusts his bandana, then takes it off and ties it back on again.

"Playing it cool?"

"Girl, I didn't even know he liked guys until last night!"

"Maybe he didn't know, either."

"Oh, he knew."

"Gross. I think."

"Anyway, I don't want to freak him out."

"That's bullshit."

"That's rude."

"Can I ask you something?" I'm just starting to smell the coffee; a little puddle of it is forming at the bottom of the pot. Rafael shrug-nods. "Does your mom know you're gay?"

Even I'm not sure where the question comes from. It's none of my business, really. I thought I was avoiding the tough conversations before, but I've stumbled effortlessly into another one.

Rafael doesn't seem to mind, though. At least, the question doesn't make him twitchy and nervous like it's making me. He just shrugs and starts picking at the sugar packet again. "I don't know. I never really tried to hide it from her. I think she caught on."

I wonder if my dad would ever just *catch on* to the fact that I'm asexual. Probably not. And that's probably fine. He might notice me crushing on girls. I mean, if I ever expressed interest in more than one girl. If I ever expressed interest in more than one person, period.

Don't be into Mei.

Right.

I wonder if Joseph texted me back. I wonder if he's mad.

"She's cool with it, then?" I ask Raf. He's tapping a fingernail against the coffee pot and I feel like we're on the same page: never staying on the same page for too long. I've forgotten what we were talking about and come back to it a million times between now and the last thing Rafael said.

"Huh? Yeah. I think so. Yeah." He crouches down so he's eye level with the coffee pot. "This coffee is gonna be shit, Callie, definitely not worth the wait."

"You shouldn't *play it cool with Jian*, Raf."

"Psh!" He swats his hand in my direction. "Respect my game, C."

"Yeah, all right."

We watch the coffee in silence, and I can't stop thinking about Joseph. He's definitely still mad. Rafael asks, "You still messing around with Joseph?"

"No!" I shove my hand into the pocket where my phone usually is. "We're not messing around."

"Are you hanging out, though?"

"I—" Are we? I don't know if I'd consider a brief stint in some guy's basement 'hanging out.' I also don't know what Rafael thinks 'hanging out' means. I just say, "Yeah. But like, casually."

"Okay."

"What?"

"I don't know." Rafael rearranges the stack of plastic coffee cup lids. "Do you want to be hanging out with him casually?"

"Yeah!" No. Not really. Shit, why do I sound so defensive? Raf quirks an eyebrow my way. "Look, we're not, like, dating again or anything. Just..."

"Hanging out."

"Casually." I *casually* try to look at everything inside Martin's All-Night Gas and Grub besides Rafael, and it is easily the least casual thing I have ever done. My eyes finally land on a cooler of drinks and I cross behind Rafael to grab a can of sweet tea. Mei loves this stuff. I'll give it to her next time I see her.

Not long after, the coffee's done and I'm starting to feel tired and kind of antsy at the same time. I don't like when Raf and I get like this. It's not quite passive-aggressive; there's just a lot we're not saying. I can feel it and it's exhausting and scary and I'm never sure how to make things go back to normal.

I don't think Dad is done with work yet, and I don't want things to be weird between Rafael and I for the rest of the weekend. But I pay for the coffee (it is indeed total shit) and the tea in loose change and head towards the door.

Rafael walks me there, "Cause I'm a total gentleman," he says (although he doesn't say much else) and I'm hoping, but doubting, he feels as fine as he's acting.

I should say something about Kyle. About the new bruises. About being safe. Or even reassure him about Joseph. That everything between him and me is okay. I'm not sure which words would bring Raf and I back to normal, though, so all I can manage as we step outside is, "Um. So. You're all right? With everything at home—"

"Jesus, Callie!" Rafael says. He's smiling, too bright and too sudden. "You worry for nothing all the time. It must be exhausting to be you."

Something like exhausting, I suppose.

The TV is still on above the register as I push through the cold-glass door to leave. Whatever news story they're running now has nothing to do with monsters, or the lake, or the woman talking about what she saw. It hits me now that I didn't even see what her name was. I want to know more about her. I want to talk to her (and really, I don't want to talk to that many people).

It's chilly and humid outside, and it smells like it might rain. Maybe Dad'll know something about the report. If other people have seen a monster in the Lake, I'm betting the labs will want to know about it.

As I'm tucking my arms around myself for a bit of warmth, I notice the drunk guy is still hanging around outside, lit up by the flickering light over the trash can. I try not to look in his direction, but I have to pass him to get home. He mumbles something. Maybe at me. Maybe at nothing. I don't know. I remember suddenly that I don't have my phone with me, and it makes my heartbeat speed up.

I wonder if Kyle was drunk last night when Rafael came home, and I wonder if drunk guys make Rafael just as nervous as they make me. This guy outside Martin's might not be dangerous. Really, he might just be drunk.

Rafael is Catholic so I send up a prayer just for him as I make my way back down the hill. May he never run out of coffee or have to interact with an angry drunk man ever again.

14

PIRATES

I WAKE up groggy and gross-feeling, which is a spectacular way to start the day. It's already past nine, which I guess isn't late, but I feel unproductive already and I haven't even been conscious for a full minute.

Joseph hasn't replied to my message yet, which makes me feel like shit for no reason. I send him a quick, *hey, good morning.* Not that I really want to. I just feel kind of bad about leaving last night. I don't even know why. It's like I owe him something.

Dad isn't awake yet, so I throw a simple breakfast together. Toast and eggs. Routine. The doctors all said routine is usually very effective. With Dad, that's definitely the case. Eggs and toast? That's routine. Fifteen-hour work days with glorified power naps in between? That is not.

When the toaster finally goes off, Dad is shuffling into the kitchen, already dressed for work, though not super professional-looking. His beard is coming in more, and it looks too scruffy to be intentional. His shirt is tucked in but too baggy. When he sees me, he smiles, but all I can see are the dark circles around his eyes. He just looks stretched thin. He's obviously been working too much.

I don't buy that smile for a second. I don't even think he does. When you know people pretty well, I think you can tell the state of mind they're in as soon as you see them. Even if you can't describe it, I think you know. And as soon as he walked in, I could tell Dad was on edge. A few notches off from his baseline.

By the time I'd gotten home last night, Terry hadn't texted me back. That could be a good sign, honestly, but it feels like a bad one.

I won't push. Not right now.

"Work today?" he asks me.

I shake my head. My plate is empty. His food isn't even half gone.

"I've got some errands to run this morning if you don't need the car for anything."

"No, you're good to have it," I tell him.

I hate this. It's so weird. He's not himself. Or maybe he is himself and it's stressing him out. If I could know anything in the world, I would want to know how to make this easier for him. And it's totally, totally selfish. I don't know what to do or how to make this easier, and that kills me. I want things to be normal and I want to understand what's going on. This feels too much like the way Rafael and I left things last night. There's too much unsaid and no one willing to say it.

Dad doesn't say much more before he leaves. He doesn't eat much more, either. I don't say anything about that, even though I want to. I want to ask about the woman I saw on the news last night at Martin's, but I can't bring myself to bring it up. He leaves for work without much fanfare and I'm in an empty house again. Ugh.

This is constantly my life: not doing enough, then doing slightly more and feeling like I'm doing too much. It's like that with my dad, and it's like that with Rafael. I want to help. But I don't know if I even really can.

I put a DVD into my dad's old desktop computer in the living room (*Perks of Being a Wallflower,* a classic Artsy Kid movie) and try to do homework on the couch, but I end up doing about three thousand other things. I try to look up some answers for my statistics homework, but they're the kind of problems you can't easily type into a search bar. I read a blog post about meal prep for people with eating disorders and make a mental list of ingredients to pick up.

I search *Pennsylvania Lake Monsters* on my phone and get a bunch of search results that convince me I'm absolutely off-base as far as having one in my backyard goes. In vain, I attempt to find footage from the news report Raf showed me at Martin's, but it's not on Channel 8's website, and I don't know enough details to try and find it elsewhere.

For a while, I scroll through the bulletins for some of the schools Mei is looking at. The performing arts places never have pre-med tracks, but the more generalized schools don't put much time into their dance programs. I don't know how she's going to make it work. I mean, I know she will. Of course she will. It'll be tricky, but I don't think that really bothers her.

I'm productive. But not the good-grades kind of productive— the burn-through-a-ton-of-time kind. It's only a little helpful.

Around eleven, Joseph texts me about going to see a movie tonight—some horror thing I skip the ads for on YouTube—and I really don't want to go, but I tell him I will.

Before he responds, though, Mei texts me a million exclamation points several times before her face lights up my screen for a phone call.

"Hey—"

"So I'm super gay."

"Ah." I catch my reflection on the computer screen and I'm smiling, like, teeth and all. "For real?"

"For real, for real. Officially. It's me. I'm gay."

I lean into the scratchy couch cushions and say, "That's amazing. Tell me everything."

"Well." And this is so weird. This was not a conversation I think I ever expected to be having. "I was reading a lot about all this stuff."

"Like you do."

"I mean everything, like hardcore, Callie. I was so stressed out."

Guilt. Immediate guilt. My heart is aching with it. Of course she was stressed. I've been so shitty about all this Camila stuff. Why am I the worst? I sink into the couch, hoping it swallows me whole.

But then Mei is talking again. "So I'm doing all this research, right? Like am I bisexual or pansexual or even asexual?"

I choke on absolutely nothing.

"You good?"

"Yup," I wheeze.

Mei laughs on the other end like she isn't totally schooling me right now. Like this is easy. I know it's not. Not even for her. Which is why it's all kind of super sad.

"I was reading all these articles, and everything was so confusing, and I had no idea what was going on, like, genuinely, I was clueless. But then... okay." There's rustling around on her end and when it stops, I hear a tiny laugh and it makes lightning explode in my stomach. "Do you remember last summer, when we watched all of the *Pirates of the Caribbean* movies?"

"I do." I remember it really well because we were smashed together on her bed, streaming them from some suspicious website on her school computer, and we thought it was the funniest, most badass thing. Honestly, it totally was.

"We were right next to each other, right?"

"Right."

"Right." More shuffling. Then just quiet. Until softly, Mei says, "Yeah. I remember being right next to you. And I remember Orlando Bloom was on screen in all his pirate clothes or whatever he was in those movies. And I remember saying, 'He's so hot.' And then I remember looking over at you and you just kind of shrugged, like whatever.

"And I felt kind of ridiculous because I realized I had just called Orlando Bloom hot because honestly, that's just what you're supposed to do. It was just like, I don't know, going through the motions.

"But you didn't go along with it, I guess. You didn't

care, and maybe I'm just obsessing over that moment, but whatever. I guess it was just like, no. I didn't care about Orlando Bloom, really. Or any guy, I don't think. I was just saying he was hot. 'Cause that's what you say. Well, not you, I guess. You didn't care, and so I felt bad for pretending to care? If that makes any sense? And I just remembered that for some reason. I didn't actually care about Orlando Bloom, you know? I just said it. With guys, it's always just going through the motions."

Going through the motions. Saying yes to dates and leaning in for kisses and smiling small smiles because the timing feels right. Because that's what happens in movies. You go through the motions. It might not make sense, but how can you know what else there is to do?

So yeah, I think I know what she means. No, I'm sure that I do. And I'm filled with this feeling. This *known* feeling. I love it so much that I don't move for a little bit because I want her words to sit with me, sit around me, cover me like a blanket. Maybe I'm lonely and maybe what she said makes me not feel alone.

Going through the motions.

"That's really, really cool, Mei," I tell her. Quietly, simply, inadequately. It's really, really cool. I'm very, very happy.

"Yeah, well..." She's flustered. I can tell. Like how people get after they say something very passionately and then they aren't sure if their passion was correctly placed. In this case, it was. I think. For sure. "Also, Keira Knightley," Mei adds.

I bust out laughing and it feels really loud. It probably is. Louder than warranted at least. The kind of loud that is needed to break you out of a quiet moment, to move on and do whatever you need to do for life normally. She's laughing, too, and I push myself a bit out of the couch cushions I've sunken into.

"Thank you for telling me."

"What? About this?" Mei says. "Obviously. Who else would I tell? Shit. Do I have to tell people now? I didn't even think about that."

"You can do whatever you want."

"I want to watch *Pirates*."

I smile. Because I kind of do, too. "Do it."

15

GO TO THE MOVIE

RAFAEL STOPS BY AFTER WORK, which isn't weird. But he doesn't stay for long, which is.

That's probably my fault, since I let my worry take over and the first thing I ask him is, "Have you said anything to Jian yet?" I don't mean to be aggressive, but I think it came off that way.

All he says is, "Respect my game," and I don't think he's trying to be aggressive either.

That's it. It kind of kills me.

We're never like this. We're never tense around each other or lost for words. One time, freshman year, I stayed home sick from school, and when Rafael came by in the afternoon to drop off some of the homework I'd missed, we accidentally ended up hanging for five hours without even realizing it. That's how we are. I don't think I've ever had a conversation with Rafael that lasted for less than thirty minutes.

But right now, he's walking out the door, and I don't think we've said ten words to each other.

Of course this is the moment that Joseph's giant shiny pickup truck pulls up in front of our trailer. Of course it is.

Rafael pauses on the sagging porch. He shifts forward as Joseph shuts off the ignition. The engine is one of those ones that is always making an insane amount of noise. It drives me crazy, but the silence that comes once it's gone feels so empty and terrifying.

Rafael cuts his eyes away from Joseph and looks at me. His face is so neutral, so non-expressive, that for a second I just freeze.

"We're just going to the movies," I say, trying to stay quiet. The pickup door slams shut. Joseph leans across the hood and jerks his head in greeting.

"Sounds casual," he says, loud enough for Joseph to hear. Not that Joseph knows what we're talking about.

"Yup."

Rafael hops off the porch. The sudden movement jolts me into realizing how still he had been.

"Bye, Callie!" Rafael says. He raises his hand in a wave but doesn't look back. Just heads to his trailer without saying a word to Joseph.

I so, so do not want to talk about any of it. The weirdness. The walking away. The nervous feeling all of it leaves in my gut. And I definitely don't want to discuss it with Joseph. So I just walk across the stones and slide into the passenger seat and say, "Hey," when he situates himself behind the wheel. I smile in a way that I think is something along the lines of cute, but honestly, what do I know?

But Joseph isn't even looking at me. He's glaring at

Rafael, who's sauntering down the road. "What the hell is that guy's problem?"

God, I feel sick. Holy shit.

"Do you have a thing for him or something?" Joseph spits out. Usually, I think I'd laugh at that. But there is something so vicious and wild in Joseph's tone.

"No." I tell him. "God, no. He's—he likes someone else."

"Bullshit."

"Hey," I say again. Really trying to push *something* into my tone. Really trying to be distracting. "Hey."

Joseph finally looks at me. With the sun now fully hidden behind hills and forests, the shadows over his eyes are darker than usual, menacing. He looks at me. And I can tell; he's not angry anymore. He's something like angry and it's just as unpleasant.

He says, "Hey." It sounds dark and intentional and wrong. He adds, "Trailer trash," and I almost flinch. I almost bolt out of this stupid truck with its stupid loud engine because this is not casual. This is the opposite of casual. And there is a part of me that is small and buried and powerful that knows I want nothing to do with this.

But still, I just smile. And when he wraps a piece of my hair around his finger and tugs a bit, I just laugh.

It's what you're supposed to do. It's how you're supposed to act. And I can't stop. Even though I know that I'm doing it and I hate that I'm doing it, I just don't know what else to do. They don't show you what else to do.

The movie is at one of those drive-in theaters, which I didn't realize was the case. We have to tune the radio to a certain station and wait for it to get dark outside, and then it's just us. Me and Joseph. Joseph and me. Alone in a car together.

There are other people around—obviously there are other people here—but being in someone's car, in the dark, with the radio on for just the two of you to hear is inherently private. It's secluded in the open.

I'm feeling claustrophobic. The smell of sugar and popcorn and sweat drifts in through the windows and I hate where I am. I hate *who* I am. The opening credits aren't even over.

This isn't where I should be. Not on the day Mei literally came out. I should be with her. We should be talking about it! We should be celebrating or just hanging out in her room, eating pizza. Watching *Pirates of the Caribbean*. All of this—Joseph, the horror movie we're watching together, being in this stupid, loud truck—it feels wrong.

Mei is smart, obviously, and methodical about understanding whatever she thinks needs to be understood. But smart people need to feel supported. And I want her to feel supported. I want her to know I support her, especially right now. Right now, I need to be with her. Maybe that would mean helping her figure out whatever it is that's happening between her and Camila. And if that is what supporting Mei means, then okay. I'll do it. I will. It hurts. It hurts. But I will.

But if I'm all hung up on Mei, with whatever crazy romantic, possibly non-sexual feelings I have towards her, I can't do that.

So I settle back into the fake leather seat, because maybe movie night with Joseph is better than movie night with Mei. Maybe moving on—being normal—is the best way I can support her.

It's not her fault I can't figure out what I'm feeling, or, maybe, what I'm not feeling. I need to get over it. Or at least ignore it for a bit. At least until prom. At least until I can get over it for real. This is about Mei. This is about my best friend.

I need to get over my own issues.

"Are you gonna be scared, Catwell?"

Joseph nudges me with his hand and lets it drop back down onto the seat between us. He's got one of those trucks where the front seat is just one long undivided bench. It's very inviting. Ugh.

The answer is yes, of course. For some reason, having the audio right in your face is way more invasive than normal, gigantic movie-theater speakers. I realize I haven't said anything for too long, which I guess Joseph takes as a sign that I am far too terrified to even speak. He shifts closer to me on the bench and puts an arm around my shoulder. He leans down until his lips are practically brushing against my ear.

"I've got you. No worries."

Possibly the least comforting thing I've ever heard. Possibly the opposite of comforting. Internally, I'm squirming away.

Externally, I say, "That's good."

Because if it has to be like this, if it has to be me and Joseph, Joseph and me, then it'll be like going through the motions.

The movie keeps rolling, people keep walking by outside to get popcorn, and I'm letting him touch me.

Because that's what you do. I'm letting him lean even closer to me because I'm supposed to like this. It's who I'm supposed to be.

I don't like horror movies, but I'm starting to realize that doesn't even matter, because I haven't been able to pay attention to a single thing on screen. The arm that Joseph has around my shoulder slips down until his hand is on my waist, moving in slow, ridiculous circles that make me want to jump out of the car.

Why the hell would I want that?

Why the hell am I the way that I am?

I like Mei. I like being around her, being close to her. Why can't I be like that with Joseph? Why can't I like the things I'm supposed to like?

I can tell that he wants to kiss me. I can feel his eyes glancing my way even though I'm looking very deliberately at the screen. If I move, even a bit, I think he'll go for it.

What would he do if I told him I'm asexual?

I pull my legs up against my chest and wrap my arms around them. Joseph shifts away a bit. It's a small relief. I'm still here. With him. This is still happening.

"Callie, come on, what's the problem?"

Of course he can tell I'm uncomfortable. I'm unsubtle. I'm dramatic.

"I just don't like this kind of stuff." I wave my hand at the screen. "This horror stuff."

"You wanna get out of here?" he asks. I hate that question. I absolutely despise it. Because I can't pull the same move twice. I can't just run away this time.

"Um."

Joseph scoots closer to me again and slouches down so our eyes are level. They're so dark. His eyes. Always covered in shadows, even in the glaring light from the movie screen. It's like he's always wearing sunglasses. Always has a secret. "Seriously," he says. "I don't mind."

I'm sure he doesn't.

"Um." Jesus, I've forgotten how to speak. Joseph isn't looking at me anymore. Well, he is. He's looking at my lips, shifting closer just a little. Bit by bit.

And all I can think is that this is what it means to go through the motions. All I can think is that I'm going to let him kiss me because I'm too scared to tell him not to. All I can think is that this is happening, this is happening, this is—

Everyone shrieks. Both of our eyes cut to the movie screen where there is a lot of blood and a lot of agonized tears. I haven't been following the plot. I don't know the context of all this, and I don't really care. Before Joseph has a chance to look back at me, I'm as far away as I can get. I'm leaning against the passenger side door of the truck and he puffs out an annoyed kind of sigh and I hate myself. I think I really, really do.

We stay pretty far apart for the rest of the movie. Still, I couldn't tell you the title, or basically anything that happened on screen. That's pretty normal for me. If there is something I'm supposed to be focusing on, I definitely won't be able to focus on it. Especially when things are so weird and tense. I spend most of the runtime staring out the window, like Joseph's truck is actually moving and I'm watching the landscapes blowing by, while feeling guilty and useless and pathetic. Joseph doesn't try to do anything again. He doesn't try to talk to me, either.

When I pull something like this—something like avoiding a kiss—it takes exactly two seconds for the guilt to set in. I can feel Joseph fuming across from me, and I feel like shit because it's my fault that this night is going so badly.

We're starting to feel like we did before. When it was Joseph and Callie. The couple. I'm starting to feel like I did when I was with him before and it's just bad; it's all bad.

When the screen goes dark and people start turning on headlights and making their way towards the exit, he looks at me for a while and still stays quiet. We're quiet the whole way home and I try not to make too much noise picking at my nails. I'm not sure what time it is or what homework I have to cram in before I try and fall asleep. By the time we pull into Lake View and Joseph parks in front of my place, my ears are roaring from the lack of conversation.

It's whatever. I tried. I did. I guess I'll keep trying. I want this to be normal. I want to make sense. But right now, I'm just getting out of the truck, not saying anything, not trying to make right the million things I did wrong. Tomorrow I'll feel guilty about how this all went down all over again. But I'm tired right now. And I can't bring myself to try and fix anything. I don't have the energy.

When I hear Joseph's door opening opposite of me, I feel a fresh burst of nerves hit my chest because I'm absolutely exhausted. He's not staying in the car, and it'll take everything out of me to try and play along with whatever he's trying to do now.

We walk to the door.

I undo the lock.

He leans against the handle before I can grab it.

"Do you want to take this slow or something?"

It takes me a second to really realize what he's talking about. Us? Do I want to take *us* slow? And that gets me. Because I don't want to take this relationship—whatever this is—anywhere. That wasn't the question, though. "I guess."

Joseph laughs once. A breathy 'ha' while rolling his eyes. "You guess."

"I don't know, Joseph," I say. And I see how this conversation is supposed to go. I'm supposed to apologize and give some reason for ignoring him the way that I did.

I'm not used to this whole relationship thing.

It was a long day.

The movie was just stressing me out.

But none of that is true. And besides, I know what he wants. I just say, "I was nervous, I guess."

"About what?"

"About..." And I can't believe myself. I really can't. I'm tired. I want this night to be over. And yet...

Go through the motions. Go to the movie, hold his hand, lean into his side, like the smell of his cologne, let him walk you to the door.

Before you go inside and say goodnight, push up on the balls of your feet, look at his mouth, grab his shirt.

Kiss him.

I kiss him and I let him kiss me back, and I don't

think about how I want to be away from it. How it's too much. How I never wanted this. We never *talked* about this. I don't think about any of that and I certainly don't say it. So why would Joseph notice any of it?

It's a quick kiss. A simple one. An expected one. And when he pulls away and looks down at me, he's smiling. Like he just won some game. He just *won* me.

I swallow. "Goodnight."

"Night, Catwell."

As he saunters away, I go inside and curl into the couch, and I watch his truck pull away from the window. That's what you're supposed to do.

You go to the movie. You give him a kiss.

You crawl into bed and you try not to cry.

16

POWERFUL

TRULY, I cannot believe that it is Monday and I have to do this whole week all over again, just like I did the last. Exhausting. Tiring. Boring.

And I can tell it's going to be a scattered day. My brain is buzzing. Too much happened yesterday, and I definitely did not do several assignments that I'm sure are due in less than an hour. When I finally manage to roll out of bed, it's way too late to meet Rafael for coffee and I hardly have time to sit down with Dad. He wasn't home last night when Joseph brought me back. I think he was at work, but I don't want to ask.

"Are you working on homework right now?"

"Uh." Yes. For, like, three different classes.

Dad just says, "Callie."

And I just say, "Dad." He pulls a page of my statistics work towards him and frowns at it. Yikes.

This is good, though. I think looking over my bad homework distracts him enough from breakfast that he can actually let himself eat it. But by the time I'm finishing up a reflection sheet on *Beowulf*, he hasn't eaten a ton and I don't trust him to keep going if I'm not there.

I think he notices. I think he always notices that I'm stressed and worried about him and I think it kills him a little, but honestly, that just makes me more stressed. Vicious cycles.

But right now is an okay moment. Fragilely okay, but still, in essence, *okay*.

There's something I've been meaning to ask him. "Have you seen the stuff they're running on channel eight recently?"

He glances up from the math problem he was scowling at. "... The weather?"

"Yeah, yeah." I shuffle some papers around because I don't want to look like this is something I care too much about. But ever since I saw that report Rafael showed me at Martin's, I haven't been able to shake the thought of the woman describing exactly what I saw in the lake.

I go on, trying for casual (and probably failing).

"I meant, like, the local news segments. Like..." I look up and Dad is looking right at me now. "There was that woman who was talking about a— a lake monster, or something that she saw. Did you hear anything about that? At work?"

"Huh." Dad sits back and scratches at the scruff on his jaw. "Lake monster sightings? They get those sometimes."

"They do?"

"Yeah. I mean, you know how it is around here."

"Sure." I do know how it is around here. I know that we're a small town, but our draw is the mysterious lake and the woods and the labs that sit in the middle of them.

The mystery of what all of those things have to do with each other. There are a lot of speculations and theories that buzz around. But this one is different. At least, it is to me. "This lady seemed to have, like, specifics, though. She sounded legit."

"I'll have to ask around." Dad sits forward again and squints at me, and maybe he catches that I'm being weird. He's always been able to catch that. "Usually, with claims like that... I don't know, I guess the tendency is to not believe them?"

"Oh." I hear the disappointment in my own voice. I know I'm invested in this, but I shock even myself with how hurt I sound.

"It's just hard to believe that they could all be true," Dad says.

"Well, what if they are true?"

"Hey, I'm just the secretary." He chuckles and it feels like he's testing me, trying to get a feel for where I'm at. So I laugh back, but I feel uneasy, embarrassed again for some reason, like when Martin called that lady dramatic.

I should be wrong here, right? I should be agreeing with what Dad is saying. But I don't and it feels shitty. It feels ridiculous.

And of course, Dad catches on. "If something does end up being true, though... I don't know Callie. Usually with anything strange or controversial, they just kind of try to deal with it quietly. Not a lot of media attention, you know?"

"Right."

I don't know why any of this bothers me. If I did see that lake monster—and maybe I really did—then who cares, really, if a bunch of people don't believe it? That's good, I guess. A lake monster is the kind of thing that was made to be a secret. Something special.

And maybe that's it. It's that feeling. That *special feeling*. I feel it like a crazy and wild part of me. Magic or strange science or just a pocket of nature that kept itself hidden until I got to see it. Something about seeing that monster—it felt vital to me. Pink eyes, shimmery scales, swimming in forest-green water that reflected the trees and the mountains and the skies. Old magic.

That's what seeing the lake monster felt like and that's what I remember when I think about her, and that's why it's hard to hear that it's not true. That it's not something worth exploring. That it's not something worth believing.

It sounds crazy, but I feel like a part of me is just getting... discounted.

Dramatic. Crazy. Unbelievable.

Me.

But it can't be that complicated; it's simple. There is something in the lake or there is not. Either way, I think I saw it. That's just how it is, that's just what it is. Something that may or may not exist.

I hurry through the rest of my homework and try to carefully stow it away in my bag (wrinkled *and* incorrect is such a bad combination). My dad quirks an eyebrow as I make my way to the door.

As I shrug my backpack over my shoulder, I say, "A lot of this stuff is just graded on completion. So." I shrug.

"That's the spirit."

"Okay." I glance at his plate. "I'll see you. Text me. Or, I mean, I'll text you and Terry."

"Have a good day, Callie."

Yeah. Probably not. What can you do?

Rafael isn't on the bus, which puts me even more on edge. I try texting him, but by the time we pull up to the school, I still haven't gotten a response. I did get a text from Joseph—a few, actually. One from last night after he left. It's just a bunch of winking faces, which I actually do react to. I'm cringing. I can see my reflection in the phone screen. He sends one now.

Meet at your locker?

And then more winking faces. Ugh.

Ugh. Ugh. Ugh.

Thankfully, Mei is at my locker when I get to school. She's got some kind of energy that repels Joseph, which I don't understand but respect greatly. She's at my locker and she's beaming.

"Hey, hey buddy." She punches at my arm lightly, so I punch at hers.

"Feisty," I say.

And then she's hugging me, quick and fast and energetic. When she pulls away, she says, "I'm a new woman, I swear. I'm bolder. I might get into boxing?"

"Please do."

I'm laughing. I always am with Mei. I fish out the can of iced tea I got last night and hand it to her. "Cheers?"

"To being gay!" She takes it from me and raises it high in the air. She's not being quiet or anything, and some people definitely look our way. All I can do is laugh. With Mei, life is better. Life is the best. So when a certain question comes to mind, I really don't want to ask it. I remind myself that I need to be supportive. I really do.

"So. What does this mean as far as—I mean, for you and Camila." I'm fiddling with my lock but not paying attention to what numbers I put in. "Like, are you going to go to prom with her, then?"

"Oh." Mei leans against the locker next to mine and I look over to her. She's got on this bright red cropped sweatshirt and lipstick that matches it just a shade away from perfectly. I can't really read the expression on her face, but it's a little stressed. There's this tiny wrinkle between her eyebrows. "Well, all of this had me thinking—"

"Catwell!" I feel my arms tense up immediately. Down the hallway a bit, across from us, Joseph is leaning against the wall and smirking at me.

"Hey," I say. It sounds quiet to me, but Joseph still jerks his head, like *come over here*. I really don't want to. He really does keep at least a five-foot radius around Mei and, as much as that makes Mei look really cool, it makes the prospect of going over and talking to Joseph feel kind of intimidating.

"Callie?" Mei is frowning at me with her eyebrows and I don't really know what to make of it. "Is this happening again?" Mei asks, voice hushed.

"I don't—no. Not really. Maybe."

"Oh. Oh, okay. You just seemed—like, last time we talked about it..." Her whole face screams disappointment. She thinks this is a bad idea. Me and Joseph. Joseph and me.

"Yeah. I don't know." I can feel Joseph staring at me and I hate it. "I should probably go talk to him."

I do go over to Joseph. And I'm kind of frustrated

because I was talking to Mei and I would definitely *rather* be talking to Mei, but here I am, standing in front of him instead.

Joseph doesn't even say hi. He just grabs my waist and pulls me towards him and kisses me, and I'm honestly so shocked by it that for a second, I can't even pretend to not be horrified. I pull away and he's smiling down at me as I look around and try to breathe. I think some people are, like, cheering for us or something.

Mei is by my locker and watching us, still frowning, but then Camila comes up to her. And I don't know what she says—I can't tell—but it gets Mei to smile. Bright and real. She's smiling. Not frowning. Not worrying about me. And I love that expression on her. I think I could look at it forever. Except I'm here with Joseph, wanting to be anywhere else.

"I have to go to statistics." Seriously. Anywhere else. Even a half-full math classroom.

"We've got like, ten minutes until the bell—"

"Gotta talk to my teacher." I'm walking off. I don't have to talk to my teacher. Well, maybe I do. I don't know. It doesn't matter. I don't think I breathe or blink or hear any of the normal hallway chatter. I'm just walking. Walking until I'm sitting in my desk at the back of the classroom, existing in some dumb combination of angry and scared and just completely lost. But away—away from Joseph and away from Mei, who is interested in another girl.

Selfish.

Selfish, selfish, selfish.

People start to trickle in. Morning conversations build

on top of each other, getting louder as the minutes tick by. I wait for Rafael to show up, but he never does. I text Terry even though I don't think she starts working until later. She won't mind another message from me. Right?

I scroll through all my texts from Joseph, trying to figure out if I was being too flirty or something. Or maybe not flirty enough. I can't tell. I don't know what I'm trying to do here. I just know that I'm not doing it right. I'm not what he wants me to be, but I'm not what I want to be, either. I'm not anything.

The final bell rings, and Rafael still isn't here. I haven't heard anything from my dad or Terry, and I can't get Mei's face out of my mind. Her, smiling, becoming bright because of Camila. I can't stop feeling Joseph's hand on my waist in the hallway. I can't stop thinking about how everybody could see us.

I can't concentrate, and it's not just about Joseph or my dad or Mei or Rafael. It's all of those things plus a million others. Like college, and how I haven't really put any effort into trying to think about it. And the lake monster I thought I saw in Lost Lake and how she's either out there or I'm crazy. And my DVDs. I haven't touched them since I put them on my shelf, all haphazard and crazy. I'm wondering if I should move them or change them, or why it even matters. I feel like it matters. All of this matters.

And only five minutes have passed. My God. I need to not be here right now. I need to not be anywhere.

I think about the lake monster again and I try to focus on her. On that feeling of being real and relevant and simple. It was only four days ago that I saw her, but it feels like something that happened forever ago. I wonder if she remembers me. I wonder if she's real.

The day drags on forever. Just a bunch of bells ringing and lockers slamming and teachers droning. I manage to not see Joseph anymore, even in the hallways. I don't see Rafael either, and he isn't getting back to me. Terry texted me around lunch to let me know that things weren't great, but they weren't awful. Not great, not awful. That's been the pattern here for a while. It's not a great pattern.

After school, I walk to Joey's and try to be friendly and competent during my shift, but honestly, I'm kind of all over the place. We aren't too busy during the week, which is when I let things slide. If there's too much time in between taking orders and making food, I get distracted and do something dumb like forgetting to restock napkins or wipe the counters down.

Vaguely, the work I'm doing is registering in my mind, but I'm kind of in a million other places.

His hand. My waist.

Her smile. His arms.

Being at home is somehow worse. I feel like I haven't seen my dad in ages. Is he real? Is he like the monster? Maybe I made him up. It's too dim in my room—I probably need to replace the lightbulb. I just stare at my DVDs for what feels like a half hour and then wander down to the water, phone in hand. There are a bunch of texts from Mei and a bunch of texts from Joseph and I can't look at any of them.

I debate going over to Rafael's place and seeing if he's all right, but I feel like he would hate that. He would hate me. What changed? When did things between us change?

He said he was fine. He told me not to worry. So I won't worry.

Ha.

The lake is infuriatingly glassy-smooth; only small waves ripple across the surface, gently lapping at the cement. The sun is setting across Lost Lake and orange bits of light get caught in my eyes. I know it's getting kind of late and there are things I should be doing. Like homework or replacing light bulbs. But I want to go out on the lake. I think I'll take the boat out, just for a bit. Just for a second.

My phone is vibrating. Mei is calling.

"Callie?"

"Mhm."

"Hey, did you get my texts? I thought you'd need a ride home from work."

"Oh." I walked. I don't really remember it.

"... Callie? Are you at home?"

"Yeah."

"Are you okay?"

"Yeah. I'm gonna go out on the lake, I think."

"The lake? Callie, it's getting cold, it's like—it's cold, Callie. You shouldn't go out."

"I have to."

"You... Okay. Um. Can I come with you, then?"

"... No. It'll be cold."

"Yeah, you shouldn't be alone on a cold boat in the middle of a lake while a sea monster is on the loose."

"Lake monster."

"Even so."

I shift back and forth from foot to foot. The cement

is rough beneath my feet and I realize that I'm not wearing shoes. "You don't have to do this. It's stupid-crazy."

"I don't think it's stupid-crazy, Callie."

"Okay."

"Okay," Mei says.

And then I'm fine. She's powerful. She's Mei. I'm talking to Mei. I feel like I'm breathing for the first time since this morning.

"I'll be over in a bit." She sounds relieved. I think I was freaking her out. I think I was freaked out, period.

Two deep breaths. Mei is coming over. That's fresh air.

"Okay."

I sink down onto the dock and let my bare feet dangle over the water. That's weird. I focus on trying to see the little fish swimming in the shallow water in the dimming light. It honestly feels like the first thing I've concentrated on all day.

17

STUPID CONSTELLATIONS

MEI IS HELPING me heave the boat right-side up, the long grass hissing against it. There isn't much light anymore and I kind of feel bad for dragging her out here. We have school tomorrow. "So you kissed him?"

I don't know why I'm telling her about my date with Joseph yesterday. I think I just wanted to hear myself say it all and maybe tell her how much I hated the whole thing. But I don't tell her that, and apparently, I don't convey it like that either. Mei is just nodding along, taking it all in.

Maybe there was nothing to hate about the date last night. Maybe I'm being dramatic again. That's my thing.

"And then what?" she asks.

"What?" The boat thumps right-side up in the grass and we each grab an end and shuffle towards the water.

"You kissed and then what?"

"And then he went home." We get to the edge of the water and I set my end of the boat down and look at Mei. "I don't wanna, like, sleep with him."

"You don't?"

"No."

"Okay." I'm sure I'm making up the smile I hear in her voice.

I understand that this would be a good time to say, *honestly, I don't think I want to sleep with anyone, possibly ever. I think that's just who I am.* But I don't say that. I want to, but I don't. And the moment passes; I try not to think too hard about it. I'll tell her eventually. I know that I will.

It's fully dark by the time we paddle out to the middle of the lake. The plank seats are pretty uncomfortable, so we slide them out of the way and lay back on the bottom of the boat. It's cramped, or cozy. The two of us are side by side, angled slightly towards each other because this is a boat and this one is tapered. It's the kind of setup that might not be comfortable in twenty minutes, but it's comfortable now.

It's also the kind of setup that isn't ideal for people on the lookout for mysterious creatures in a lake, as we are one hundred percent facing the sky. But I can't bring myself to mind that bit.

Mei breathes deep and blows air out of her lips like she's smoking or something.

"Long day?" I ask.

"I guess." She wiggles like she's trying to nestle farther down into the boat. "I thought maybe you were having a mental breakdown there for a second."

"I think maybe I was."

We both laugh, but Mei nudges my shoulder and says, "Callie! I'm serious. I know we talked this morning but that was it. It felt so weird. I didn't realize how much we usually talk."

"Too much?"

"Never too much."

"All right." Above us, stars are starting to shine, and it *is* getting cold out here. "I'm sorry."

"For what? For nothing. You're totally fine. I was just worried about you," she says. I don't deserve her. "Joseph doesn't seem like... I guess he just makes me nervous. I don't know why."

He makes me nervous too. But for now, I don't really want to get into any of that. I tell Mei, "You make *him* nervous."

"Good."

I think about asking her about Camila, but I can't bring myself to do it. I can't bring myself to make this moment about more than us. I'm selfish. I'm ridiculous.

"I was looking at some of the schools you were talking about," I say instead. "You picked the weirdest programs to double major in."

"Shut up." She laughs and hits my stomach with the back of her hand. She lets it rest there, right under my rib cage. "I don't know if that's what I want to do, anyway."

"What?" I almost look over to her, but I don't think we have the room for that. "Why? You seemed excited before."

"I was! I am still, I think. It's all just a lot. To think about and, like, figure out. How the hell are we supposed to figure this out?"

"You know, not all physical therapy programs require a bachelor's degree."

"Yeah..."

"I guess most do."

"And I want to study bio, like, genuinely, I do. It's just... I don't know. I want to do other things too. I want to do a million things."

"Me too." My voice is so soft— so hardly there—that it doesn't sound like mine. Which makes sense. It's not something I really expected myself to say.

"I want to know everything," Mei says.

"One day, I think you will."

The backs of her fingers shift, one after the other, like she is tapping piano keys in the air. I'm obsessed with the way we fit together right now and the way that Mei's shoulder pressed against mine is the only source of warmth I can feel. I'm obsessed with us.

My heart hurts.

"Okay." Mei shifts around a bit until her head is kind of leaning on my shoulder. I can barely see it in the corner of my eye, but her hand opens and before I even think about it, my fingers are threaded through hers. She says, "Can you point out constellations for me? Like we're some of the artsy kids from your movies."

"Oh, yeah. Sure, sure." I clear my throat. Mei laughs. The hand that she's holding feels otherworldly. Right now, it feels magical to hold Mei's hand. I point up at the sky. "You see that cluster over there? All the bright little stars?"

"Yes."

"Yeah. That's one of my favorites," I tell her. "They call that one, Hercules' Dick."

"Okay." She's chuckling. Trying not to full-on laugh,

which is fair, but I don't have the self-control. "Oh my God, Callie."

I'm cackling and then Mei is too; she's turned into my shoulder and I can feel the puffs of her breath against my neck and that makes it all so much worse, and so much better. Amidst it all, she somehow says, "You're like a sixth-grade boy." Which makes me laugh even harder. It's that kind of cackling that makes your sides hurt, in the good way. I've got Mei's hand in a viper grip.

I think I am literally rocking the boat right now.

"That's exactly what I'm always going for."

And I don't feel like I'm anywhere. I feel like I'm with Mei and that's it. There's sky above us and we're bobbing in the water below, but mostly it's just her and me. I feel warm from the laughter, from being next to Mei.

When I turn my head to look at her, she's already there, already looking at me.

You'd think it'd be difficult, in the lack of light here, to really make out the color of someone's eyes or the little details of their face. But we're close. Really close. And I can see Mei totally. There is so much to her. Her eyelashes are kind of short and kind of perfect. The eyeliner she had on all day is faded and smudged around her eyelids. When she blinks, it's like the whole world shifts and then falls back into place. There is the sky and it's kind of an infinite feeling and there is Mei, and she feels the same way. Endless and forever. Like a constellation. A real one.

I'm being dramatic. I know that I am. But you have to know this: when you're staring at someone you care about, drama doesn't even exist. Only they do. It's only Mei. It's always Mei. "Your eyes are pretty."

I was thinking it, but Mei said it. She said it about me. I want to laugh or something but we're so close. I try to laugh, but it just comes out like a breath.

"If we were in a movie," she says, "you'd have an eyelash on your cheek. Like," she presses her thumb lightly to the bone under my eye, "right there."

"Okay."

"And I'd tell you to make a wish." She drags her thumb across my cheek. She's practically whispering.

"I'd wish for more wishes." I'm practically whispering too. Not because we have to be quiet, but because we don't have to be loud.

"Brilliant."

She's kind of cupping my cheek in her hand and her fingers are so light on my face and all I can think about is her.

If this is love, love is easy; and it *is* easy. Being with Mei is the easiest thing in the world. But I guess it's more complicated than just being with her. There are reasons this can't happen. There's Camila and there's Joseph and there's me, who is afraid to come out because I'm not even sure if I understand what I want to come out as.

I think that if this was a movie, and Mei told me to make a wish, I'd wish that I could look at her forever—to never have to stop.

Romantic. Stupid. Whatever. They can write it on my grave: *she was romantic and stupid and never figured out what any of it meant*. Because if I'm looking at Mei, it's a different world. Everything is this moment and only this moment.

Her.

Me.

Us.

Right now, I am exactly who I want to be. And I can't do this anymore.

I don't want to ruin this moment because I think it's the last of this that I can stand. It hurts to be around Mei when I'm pretty sure she wants to be around someone else. It hits me now like a waterfall pouring straight onto my heart.

This is it. This is all we can have. I want to be fine with it. I want to be supportive. I don't think I can be those things. I think I'm kind of terrible.

With a ridiculous amount of effort, I look away from Mei and I look back up at the stupid constellations (I couldn't point a real one out to save my life). I have no idea what time it is, but it's probably too late to be awake and out on a boat when we've got school tomorrow. I sit up and the boat sways. I feel dizzy for probably about a thousand reasons, least of all the change in position.

Mei says, "All right?"

And I nod. "All right."

We head back to the trailer and hug at the doorstep, and when she drives away, I watch, and it's because it really sucks to see her go. It really sucks.

Maybe I'll be normal in the morning.

18

DEAD ENDS

RAFAEL STILL ISN'T in school today, but I've gotten one message from him.

Sick. Back soon.

If he says so.

I kind of can't stop thinking about last night with Mei. I don't know what it was. Probably some weird algae messing with my brain. Making me think I'm in love or something wild like that. I'm not in love. I don't think I am. Or maybe I have been for the past six years of my life.

When did extraordinary become my normal?

Whatever. Our class schedules don't line up, so it's not too difficult to avoid Mei. Not that I'm trying to avoid her. My whole body just kind of hurts when I'm around her, and I can't stop wondering if she's thinking about Camila or maybe some other girl I don't know about. Which is selfish. I know it is. But I don't want to drag her down. Mei can make friends like I can make sandwiches (incredibly and suspiciously quickly), and I don't want to get in the way. For the record, this is always something I thought was stupid and probably made up. Wanting to distance yourself from someone you love, just because they're interested in someone else? That still feels like a stupid kind of way to think, but it's bigger than that, I guess. It's closing some kind of emotional brain space. It's like, if I let myself think that this—me and Mei, Mei and me—is a possibility, it's all I'll think about. And it's not really a possibility, is it? It feels wrong to be friends with her when I think I want to be something else. Something romantic? I don't even know.

It's certainly not something I can think about now. Not when I'm pretty sure Mei is into Camila Flores. Not when I've got bigger, stranger things to worry about. On paper, almost anything is bigger and stranger than having a stupid crush you don't know how to deal with. But really, maybe there's nothing bigger and stranger than that.

When I get home from work, Dad is sitting at our kitchen table. He's not doing anything, just sort of staring at his hands. When he looks up at me, it's like he's reacting to things two seconds behind when they're actually happening. I have no idea what he's about to say to me, but I can feel how much I probably won't like it.

"Sup?" I toss my backpack into the corner and sit down across from him. I'm trying to be casual. Maybe this is casual. Maybe I'm reading into things. But then Dad clears his throat. He shifts in his seat and shuffles various, non-related papers on the table into a neat pile. This seems like it's going to be a negative conversation. Maybe something about my grades. I mean, he really did see *all* my homework yesterday, and I truly have no motivation to step it up in that arena.

"Callie." He clears his throat again, and I watch his eyes because he won't meet mine. I shift a bit in my seat and sit on one of my legs. Wind blows; our windows rattle. The kitchen light isn't on right now and I'm just realizing that it usually makes a buzzing noise. It feels way too quiet. "We need to talk about Terry."

"Terry from work?" She texted me at lunch to let me know all was well... Was all not well?

"I know she gave you her number, but—"

"But—"

"Just wait. Just a second." He's holding up both of his hands like he's got to make peace between us. I wonder what my face looks like. It feels like it looks freaked out. It feels like my eyebrows are too high—like they're trying to jump off my forehead. Dad says, "I know this is difficult. Me being at work so much. I know it's weird and maybe not the best, but... I'm doing fine, Callie. I promise you I'm doing fine. And Terry doesn't mind that you check in with her now and then, but..."

I feel chills everywhere. My whole body sinks. "She doesn't want me to text her so much."

"No. It's not like that." Dad runs a hand through his scruffy hair. It's light brown and sort of graying. Graying more than I realized. "She's happy you feel that you can reach out to her. And I'm thankful for that. We just—I just don't want you to feel like you *need* to check in all day. I don't want you to be worried, okay?"

"I'm not—" I can't understand this conversation. Not be worried? He just admitted none of this was ideal. What am I supposed to do? Act like I'm not thinking about this in some capacity twenty-four seven? "You —ugh."

I don't know what to say. I don't know how to explain this. I probably don't even know what I'm trying to explain.

"It's okay, I know how this..." He rubs at his eyes. "This isn't a great situation for you to be in."

He makes this about me. Dad always makes this about me. He's concerned for me. That's so backwards. I've got nothing going on—nothing that warrants any kind of actual concern.

He's *not eating*.

My dad can't look at food without clamming up and isolating himself for hours on end. He can't just sit down for lunch. He can't just eat. He can't just *do* these things. *That's* concerning. That's what he should be worried about. Not working more hours and certainly not me. What have I got going on that is worth worrying over? Absolutely nothing. Absolutely nothing at all.

"Callie?"

"You really don't want me to text her?"

"I—you don't need to text Terry. You don't *need* to. Everything is okay."

"Okay."

It's not. It's so obviously not. He's wearing his work clothes—I just realized. His keys are resting by his tapping fingers. Another shift. Another night not getting enough sleep, not being on a normal schedule. Another night where it's too easy to just not get food. Not only is the kitchen light off, but the whole room is completely spotlessly clean. I've got no way to know, really, but I just have this feeling it hasn't been used all day.

It doesn't matter; I mean it obviously does. It matters more than anything and I don't know what to do. He's my *dad*. I can't tell him what to do. I can't fix this.

I just go to my room. It's shitty but I kind of don't know what else to do. Ask him what he had for lunch? I know the answer.

Eventually, I hear Dad leave. I hear the car pull away from the house, small stones pinging against the bottom of the car. I'm buried under my comforter, Mom's blanket bunched up by my head, DVDs chaotically organized at the foot of my bed. I'm just here, being uselessly unassuming, doing nothing worth worrying about. And even though Dad just told me not to, I want to text Terry. I almost do. When did that become a knee-jerk reaction? It's just what I've always done. Not doing it makes me feel funny.

I burrow deeper under the comforter until the light from my room is totally blocked out and I'm in a little cave of blankets and sheets. I scroll through my phone. It's dumb how many times I tap back into my text messages and go for Terry's name and then stop. Like I keep forgetting it's a dead end.

That's all anything is right now; a dead end.

Dad doesn't want me to bother Terry. Rafael gets jumpy if I bug him too much—especially when it's like it is now, when I can tell he wants space. I hate that he wants space.

I want to talk to Mei. Maybe not even about any of this. I just want to talk to her. I even type out a message —just a bunch of letters mashed together. Chaotic, like the colors on my mom's blanket or the DVDs on my shelf. I don't send it, though. You can't send a bunch of letters mashed together on the keyboard like that without context. It would have to start a conversation, and I can't do that. I can't. Not after last night.

I like Mei. Really. I can't mess around with her, you know? I can't do that. I can't pretend I see things the way I always did with her. That's not fair. I can't text Mei. I can't be with Mei. It's a dead end. I can't.

The thing is, when it comes down to it, there aren't many people I really talk to. And I've kind of exhausted them all. Except Joseph. There's still Joseph. And I know it's bad to keep things going with him. I know it's not great. But it's what I can do. It's Joseph. It's low stakes— for him, for me. I can't hurt Joseph; I can't drive him away or push too hard. He doesn't care about me in the ways that would allow for any of that.

Hey, wanna come over?

I send it before I can think and the tiny *whoosh* of the message going out sounds like regret. He texts back right away, like he always does.

Sure ;)

There are other ways to feel better and to not be alone. There are other options.

Tell Mei (everything).

Talk to Dad (honestly).

Check on Raf (he's not okay, I know he's not).

But I can't face any of those people. I can't.

I can't.

There's one Joseph DeLarino. There are a million dead ends.

❧ 19 ❧

FACTS

"YOUR DAD ISN'T HOME," Joseph says. It could have been a question, but he made it into a fact. He's not even through the door yet, but the patch of gravel where Dad's truck is usually parked is very clearly empty.

"No, but..." I'm beginning to realize I didn't think this through. *My dad isn't home.* What the hell am I doing inviting Joseph over to our *empty* house?

"What? Is he going to be home soon or something?" He brushes by me and into the living room, smirking as he passes. I shut the door. I take my time doing it; fiddling with the handle, listening as it clicks in and out of place. I look through the glass, and then the screen, and can just barely glimpse Lost Lake through the bushes and trees.

"No." I don't know where this is going. This would be the *wanna get out of here* portion of those other nights. This is what you do when the parents are out of town, when you have the place to yourselves.

"Why didn't you tell me?" He's poking around the

house, looking at all our stuff like I invited him in. I did invite him in. I invited Joseph here. "Shit." His voice is coming from a different corner of the house. I didn't notice he'd left the living room. "Your room looks different, Callie."

I shuffle towards my bedroom door and look into the room. It feels like I've never been here before. It feels like it isn't my space. Joseph is sitting on my bed, half-looking looking at my movie collection and scrolling through something on his phone.

When he notices me standing there, he smirks up my way.

"Why do you have so many DVDs?"

I shrug. I try to move farther into the room. Mentally, really, that's what I try to do. But I'm honestly just kind of stuck here in the doorway. Joseph taps his phone screen and some music comes on. I don't know what kind of music. It's kind of loud. He gets up.

I hear every press of the mattress, every creak in the floor, and every note in the singer's voice blaring from Joseph's phone as he shuffles towards me.

"Come on." He's whispering, but it sounds too loud. He has his hands on my waist in a second, and he's pulling me towards him in the next. And he's leaning away, pulling me with him towards the bed.

"Um."

"Come on, Catwell."

I don't really want to think about any of it, really. I don't think at all until suddenly, I'm thinking a lot. Too much, it's too much.

We're on my bed. Joseph and me. Me and Joseph. I

kind of remember getting here, I guess. I kind of recall it happening. I'm between him and the wall. Joseph, then me, then the wall. His knees are bracketing both of mine. And I hate it all. I hate the feel of his hand on my stomach and his legs brushing against mine. I hate the music he has on—it's something stupid, something *loud*. It's all too loud; the music, the touches.

The clattering of cheap plastic as my DVDs are knocked from the shelf at the foot of my bed.

"Oh shit, my bad," he mutters against my lips. But then he *keeps kissing me*. I guess I kiss back. I can't focus. The music is so damn loud. His hand keeps trailing lower and lower—

"Hey—can we just—"

"What's the problem, baby?" *Baby*. Gross. He's never called me baby. No one ever has. I hate it. His fingers are in my hair; his mouth is on my neck.

"Seriously. Joseph, seriously." I should push him away. But I'm suddenly scared, too. What would I do if he pushed back? "*Joseph*."

"Callie."

Something snaps in me. I grab his phone and try to shut off the music, turn it down. I can't get a grip on it. While the phone clatters from my hands, Joseph is laughing against my collar bone and the way he said my name won't come unstuck from my ears. *Callie*. Like a groan, like gross desire.

I can feel the DVDs on the floor, I can't get the fucking music to stop. Joseph's fingers start to slip under my shorts.

"I'm on my period!" A lie. "I feel gross." Very true.

He finally leans away, looking down at me, wedged between him and the wall. "Seriously?"

"Yeah. Sorry." I want him to leave, I want him to get away, and I want that music to stop playing. But Joseph just tilts his head up towards the ceiling and blows air out of his nose. He's annoyed.

"Well, you could still—"

Oh my God. "I just feel really sick." I can feel my heartbeat in my ears now. I know what he was going to say, but I still don't want to hear him say it. I want to fix my DVDs.

Joseph shakes his head and looks around the room like something in here will explain what the hell my problem is. The lamp by my bed is flickering. I hope more than anything in the world that it doesn't go out.

He taps through his phone and the music is off, but it still feels loud in here. It's still impossible to calm down. I sit up and pull my legs close to my chest so when he gets up, we don't even touch.

"This was kind of a bitchy move, Catwell." His voice is the loudest and the realest of all the sounds and feelings and things happening in here right now. He says it like a fact. A simple fact. I don't even think he's trying to be mean. It's just something that is true.

This was kind of a bitchy move.

I think he's right. I think it was.

He's waiting for me to say something but I can't, and I'm pretty sure that makes this whole thing even worse. What did I expect was going to happen? I invited a boy over to my empty house. Did I think we would just talk? He's waiting for me to say something. He's waiting, he's waiting.

"Sorry." I can hardly hear myself. I *can* hear that I sound like someone who is about to burst into tears. Joseph huffs, and then he leaves. And I don't think I move for at least thirty minutes. I don't think I breathe or blink or exist for at least that amount of time.

I think he put me on pause. He told me the facts.

I realize I'm crying before I realize I'm still a real person. My face is completely soaked, but I don't remember it getting that way.

I want to scream or punch something or jump into the lake or do something regrettable and crazy. But I just slide off my bed in front of my little shelf of DVDs. Only a few of them are there—the rest are on the floor. I think I'm going to reorganize them, but I don't. I watch them all for a few seconds more and feel my mom's old blanket under my hand. It was bunched up in the corner this whole time. Now I feel it rough and scratchy in my fingers.

I leave the movies on the floor and go to take a shower. When I get back to my room, there's thunder rolling and cracking outside. Lightning flashes nearby and lights up my window.

The lamp light by my bed finally flickers out, so I grab my mom's blanket and run into the living room, turning on all the lights and the desktop computer. *Perks of Being a Wallflower* is still up on the media player, so I hit play and turn the volume nearly all the way down and wrap myself in the blanket.

I don't want to cry about this stuff. It's stupid to. It's stupid.

Stupid.

Stupid.

Stupid.

20

I CAN'T FALL ASLEEP, AND THEN
I CAN

EVERYTHING HURTS. I didn't realize it was going to storm like this. It feels like the rain is beating our trailer down. Every few minutes, huge claps of thunder rattle my whole world. It wouldn't be so bad if Mei were here. That's seriously what I'm thinking. None of it would be so bad if I were with her or if I could talk to her.

I can't believe it.

I hate storms. I really, really do. I was kind of trying to fall asleep on the couch out here, but it just isn't happening. I get caught in between different states repeatedly: dream, awake. Awake, dream. I'm trying to break into one or the other, but neither will let me in.

I'm finally heading somewhere close to sleep. I'm trying to commit to it, but I can't. There's a monster in the lake outside. There's a hand on my waist. There's a knee brushing against my thigh. There's a monster. No one would believe me if I told them.

Now there's a knock at my door.

I'm sure it's Joseph. I feel this ridiculous dread; it's all that I am. I think I'm awake but really, I might not be. The knocking comes again and then a giant clap of thunder and then I hear this odd, strangled, "Callie?" And then I'm experiencing an entirely different kind of fear. The kind that reverberates in your sternum and echoes in your stomach.

It's the kind of thing that happens when you're dealing with a living thing that has been hurt.

I run to the door and wrench it open. "Rafael?" The rain is pounding violently against the lake and the stones on our driveway. I can hardly see Rafael; it's too dark, too hectic outside. But then he shifts forward. Light from the living room falls over his face. "Oh my God."

There's dark, dark blood all over his face. It's around his eyes, and on his lips. It's everywhere.

"Sorry, I should have texted—"

"Rafael... Shh. Come on, come in, come here!"

"It's not as bad as it looks." His voice is not his own. It's strange and uneven. His bright green bandana is pushed way back on his head. I grab it before it falls.

"Raf!"

I'm shaking. Why am I shaking? I set him down onto one of the chairs in our kitchen, but he stands right back up and follows me to the sink. He's not wearing shoes, just soaked-through socks. The floor creaks. Outside, thunder claps.

"Holy shit."

"Callie, just calm down. Just—"

"You actually don't get to tell me to calm down right now!" I'm talking too loudly. I know I am. My hands are moving all over the counter, trying to find band-aids or rubbing alcohol or something. "Here." Paper towels.

"Callie—"

"Just sit down. Jesus."

"No. Just me."

I nudge Rafael back into the chair and scrape another one around the table so I'm sitting across from him, wadding up paper towels, dabbing at his face. I toss the bandana onto the kitchen table. He's got on his Adidas hoodie and the red color of it looks faded behind the dark spots of blood that have dripped down onto it.

"My God." I can't find the source of the blood; the rain made it run everywhere. Holy shit. Holy shit.

"Still just me."

"Can you just—" I need to get under control. I need to breathe normally right now. "Please. This isn't—this isn't a joke."

"I know that."

"Holy shit." A flash of lightning through our window. Rafael keeps balling up his hands into fists and then letting his fingers burst out. He breathes out through pursed lips.

"Are you okay?" I ask. Obviously not.

"Yes."

"Where's your mom?"

"Out with a friend. I told her not to come home."

I try to look at him. I try to figure out what is going on. There's so, so much blood. Rafael is holding a hand over his cheek and I grab some more paper towels before gently pulling his fingers away.

"Rafael."

"Callie."

"Did—was this—did Kyle..." There's a cut on his cheekbone. All the way down to his jaw. It hasn't clotted yet. It's fresh and real and staring me in the face.

"I guess it was fucking Kyle. Jesus, Callie who cares—ow!" I'm dabbing dish soap against the wound.

"Sorry!"

"No." He takes the paper towels from me, so I move to the sink and turn on the warm water. Rafael's blood washes off my fingers. I'm too shocked to look away. He says, "I'm sorry. I just showed up, all... I don't know. And it's the middle of the night. *Fuck*."

I don't care. That's what I'm stuck on. I don't care, I don't care, I don't care. Not about it being late or him coming here. Especially if he's hurt, especially if it was someone he lives with that hurt him. But right now, I don't think I can really tell him anything.

I turn back to him and Rafael is hectic. Dabbing at his face with the paper towels and bouncing his knee up and down all over the place. In one hand he's got the bandana balled up into a fist; his fingers keep flexing and unflexing around it.

We both work to get the worst of the blood off his face, and I keep some towels pressed to the cut. I wonder if he needs stitches. I can tell Rafael is beyond crying. He's got too much energy. Nowhere to put it. Nothing to do.

"What happened?"

"It doesn't matter, Callie—"

"Seriously? No, you can't just—you can't just come here and not tell me what's—"

"He was *drunk*, Callie. He was drunk, there's nothing else to tell."

"But why—"

"Why does it matter? He's shitty and cruel and—and that's fucking all. That's fucking all. *Damn it*." Rafael rips away the towel covering the cut and little droplets of red immediately start to form along the edges of it.

I press his hand back over it.

Rafael looks at me. Our eyes are so close. Even in the dim light, I can see his eyes are such a deep brown. There's rain caught in his eyelashes and an angry crease in his brow.

He says, "I made him angry." He says it quietly. It's quieter than I've ever heard Rafael speak before.

"What do you mean?"

"It was... shit. It was so dumb, Callie." Under my hand, his fingers wriggle and move but I don't let go. "I got these flowers... ha. I got flowers from the supermarket because I was going to be back in school tomorrow and— fuck." He shifts in the chair and the floor creaks beneath him. "I was kind of going to ask Jian if he wanted to go to prom with me."

I nod. It's all I can manage. I nod and breathe and squeeze Rafael's hand.

"Kyle asked what the flowers were for and I told him. I told him I was asking someone to prom and I told him it was a boy—"

"What?"

"I told him I was asking Jian to prom."

"Why would you do that?"

Rafael leans away from me, so I sit up straight. His eyebrows are raised high. "Why not?"

"Rafael," I start. He squints at me. I'm breathless. "You don't do that. You don't put yourself in a position to—to—"

"To what? Get my face smashed up with a fucking beer bottle?"

"Is that what—"

"No one can *put themselves in that position*, Callie. No one should have any reason to expect that this,"—he rips away the paper towel and waves it between us—"is something that could happen."

"I know that..." Quiet.

"Do you?"

"Yes!" Loud. "I know that you shouldn't have to worry about this! But why give Kyle a reason to be the bad guy? Don't... give him a reason to hurt you."

Rafael laughs, and it hurts to hear it. Really, the sound hits me in the chest and makes it even harder to breathe. "He doesn't have one. Is that what you tell yourself when you're hanging around Joseph?"

All of my air is gone. "What?"

"You don't want to make *him* look shitty?"

"What the hell." I hate where this is going. I feel tears in my eyes. I'm not the one bleeding out. I'm not the one living with a monster. "That's not what—that's not the point! You're hurt—"

"Yeah! So are you! How is this any different from Joseph and you—"

"It's *different*!"

"Not really, Callie! People like Kyle—like Joseph—I

don't want to dance around people like that, Callie. I'm not here to make a bad person feel good about being terrible just so he doesn't—so he doesn't—"

"*Hurt* you."

"He's got nothing going for him! He's not in the right! I'm not going to live my life like he is."

"But you could tell someone—"

"Who? My mom? He pulls the same shit with her, Callie. He has for a lot longer. She makes excuses for him! It's not—I don't blame her or—it's just—shit, it's more complicated than just telling somebody."

"I know, but—"

"No. You don't know. You clearly don't. Because you still hang out with Joseph! You don't tell anybody that you hate being around him."

"I don't hate—"

"Callie!" Rafael cuts me off, and it hurts. It hurts because I don't know why I'm saying what I'm saying. I don't know anything, and it hurts. He says, "I can tell! I can see you, when he kisses you. I can tell you hate it; you, like—you freeze up and you don't move, and you don't say anything."

"Stop!"

"You shrink and it's not you anymore and anyone can tell that you don't want to be there, but Joseph just keeps on doing it—"

"Please, stop! Stop!"

"So why don't you pull away? Why don't you tell him to stop? I never used to get it, you know. But I figured it out. He's like Kyle. It's just like me and Kyle."

"It's different."

"It's not."

"Kyle is hurting you."

"Callie! There are a million ways someone can hurt someone else. There are a million ways! So please don't tell me to get help when you can't even get some for yourself!" Rafael is shaking. He stands up but immediately leans back against the chair like his legs cannot hold everything that he is right now. "He doesn't have a reason to be the bad guy. No one does. No one has a fucking reason to hurt anyone."

I'm not sure who he's talking about, but it really doesn't matter. I kind of want to scream, to curl up under a pile of blankets and never come out. He shouldn't say the stuff he's saying. He shouldn't compare his situation to mine. He's hiding. He's ignoring the issue. He's ignoring the issue.

"Just..." I'm quiet again. There are tears on my face and that feels so stupid and so trivial and so unfair. "Will you stay here tonight?"

It's a shitty question. Because where else would he go?

Rafael deflates and he doesn't respond. For a second it's just me sitting and him pacing a few steps across the kitchen, and then back to the table. There is nothing I understand. Nothing.

Rafael eventually points to the bathroom. "Can I... your shower?"

"Yeah."

He ducks away without saying anything else and I set a towel and some of my dad's clothes outside the door for him. Taking a seat in the recliner in the living room, I try to calm my nerves. I want to stay awake—it was so hard to fall asleep before—but my eyes keep drooping. Exhausted. Numb. That's what I am now. That's what this is. Whatever just happened, I can't process it. My brain won't let me. Nothing. Nothing is coming through.

Vaguely, I register Rafael cutting off the water and coming out to the living room. He doesn't look at me or say anything, and I stay quiet, too. In the t-shirt he's wearing, I can see his arms. They're bruised. Worse than before. Worse than I've ever seen them.

He shuts off the lights and slumps onto the couch and I want to stay awake. I don't want to dream. I don't want to fall asleep.

But sleep lets me in, and then—until the morning—I am gone.

21

ECHOES IN THE EMPTINESS

I WAKE up when Dad opens the door.

Rafael is gone.

Breathe, breathe, breathe. The chair I'm in is trying to swallow me. I can't get up fast enough. I can't breathe.

"Callie?"

It's dark outside—still dark—but getting lighter. I'm shaking. My whole body, everything in me. Shaking.

"Callie, what's wrong?"

"Where's—did you see Rafael?"

"No, Callie. Are you okay? What's going on?"

I'm on the ground, out of the chair, dizzy, shaking. Crying? Why all this crying? Rafael is gone.

"Callie." Dad is by my side, one hand on my elbow, the other on my back. We sit down on the couch—the couch that Rafael was on—and Dad says, "What happened?"

I don't know if I want to tell Dad about last night. I don't know if I should or if I shouldn't. But he asks the right questions. And I'm kind of crying through them and I think he gets it. He makes phone calls that sound very official and gives directions to Lake View, and I don't really know what's happening, just that Rafael would probably hate it.

"Last night," Dad is saying into his phone. Facing the wall, facing away from me. Like me not seeing his face somehow makes his conversation more private. Like anything could be private around here. "Yes, yes. All right. I'll be here."

I'm not sure who he's talking to. Police? Child services? I have no idea what's going to happen now. I have no idea. And it's time for school—just about time to get to the bus.

"I shouldn't go."

"Callie, you need to go to school. Sitting around here won't do any good."

"Dad—"

"Callie." He sits next to me on the couch and leans down so we're eye to eye, his hand on my shoulder. "I will update you. I will let you know what's going on, okay?"

His tone is so, so careful and I don't know what that means, except that I'm on the bus in ten minutes and Raf obviously isn't. I'm guessing he won't be in class today. I wonder if he'll be back tomorrow. I wonder if he'll be back at all. I try to figure out how much school he'd have to make up at this point. A few days, at least? That'd be a bitch. Can he even focus on something as trivial as schoolwork right now? I don't think I'd be able to.

I haven't processed a single part of what I've been doing all morning until I get to my locker and find myself struggling to put in the code. Am I really here? In school? I don't remember it happening, really. I don't remember anything that's happened, ever, until I see Mei across the hall and my pulse absolutely spikes.

Dramatic.

"Callie!"

Her voice is so ridiculously grounding. I'm suddenly very aware of everything around me. The slamming of lockers and bits of conversations, the slap of flip-flops against the linoleum, the ever-present humidity that overtakes the building around this time of year. It all comes back. Or I come back, I guess.

"Hey." There's a weird sense of relief that always comes along with seeing Mei. One that I don't feel entitled to right now, which makes sense. It shatters the second I notice who's walking beside her. "Camila, hi."

"Catwell." She nods at me and it's the coolest thing I've ever seen. She's the coolest thing I've ever seen. Her curls are loose and dramatic—dramatic in the good way, not in the me-way—and she's wearing an honest-to-god leather jacket. It's so intimidating I don't even know how to look at her.

Mei doesn't seem to, either. She keeps glancing away from Camila, meeting my eyes with a smile that's just a smidge too big. There aren't many situations that make her uncomfortable, but I guess this is one of them.

It feels like my fault. I don't know why.

"You wanna go for coffee after school or something?" she finally asks me. She's definitely uncomfortable. Camila leans against the locker next to mine and watches us. It's the kind of thing that would usually make me antsy, but I can't even manage that right now.

I've finally gotten my lock open, and I mess around

with some random notebooks that have been hanging around in here since the beginning of the semester. Then I say, "Uh. I don't, uh..." I don't want to say no, but I would feel really shitty saying yes. I want to hang out with Mei more than anything in the world, but there's also nothing that sounds more terrifying.

I know I'm being stupid. And a bad friend. But here's the thing: if I know I have a crush on Mei, it feels like I'm lying if I'm around her. It's like I'm cheating on our friendship.

"I kind of have to catch up on homework."

"Oh?" She's half smiling—waiting to see if that's a joke. It usually would be.

"Yeah."

"Are you o—"

My phone buzzes. "Hold up." It's a great excuse, and not really a fake one. There are a bunch of messages that I'm hoping to get right now. Anything from Dad or Rafael. But I check the notification and instead, to my disappointment, it's something from Joseph.

I angle my phone so Mei and Camila can't see the screen and pretend to read the text even though I don't even look at the little message preview. Just seeing his name makes me squirmy. It feels like the storm from last night got inside the school. I don't feel like myself.

"Callie?"

It's Camila that says my name, and when I meet her eyes, she seems concerned. Which is concerning. Like, we really haven't ever interacted, the two of us, and now she's looking at me like—I don't know—like she's worried.

"Yeah."

"Everything okay?"

"Yeah." I hold up my phone. "Family stuff."

Mei's eyes go wide. "Is your dad—"

"He's fine." At least, I think he is. I mean, maybe not generally, but hopefully right now.

I almost start to mention Rafael and everything that happened last night. Everything. Joseph in my room. I think my DVDs are still on the floor. All the blood. I'm surprised by how ready I am to talk about it. It's kind of freaky. I shut my mouth and my locker, though. When I turn around, Mei is still there. Camila too. They both look confused. About what? About me, probably. I'm acting weird.

"Bye." I half-salute, half-wave. I'm acting weirder. So I leave after mumbling something else along the lines of *goodbye*.

That text from Joseph makes me feel like there's something burning in my pocket where my phone is. I really don't want to read whatever he sent, but leaving it unread is just putting off something inevitably dreadful.

In statistics, Raf's seat next to me is empty. We all get graded tests back (I forget when we even took this one) and I accidently catch a glimpse of the one on his empty desk. I got a sixty-three. He got a ninety-eight.

I know Rafael is smart, but only because of stuff like this. Only because I've accidently seen a grade or stumbled across his name on the academic achievements list in the library. For such an outgoing person, there's so much about Rafael that's hard to figure out. He's got so many secrets, and I don't understand why he keeps some of them. Maybe it's a habit.

I miss him. I miss him so much because the way things are between us right now isn't right. Last night was not right and it's all I can think about.

Across the room, there's a group of boys laughing loudly— too loudly— which is normal. I usually tune it out, but my brain catches onto something one of them says.

"Lake monster."

Ah.

"She saw one?" one boy says. My heart stops.

"It was on channel eight," another replies. "She *said* she saw one."

"That's what she said." A chorus of *Ay!!!*'s.

"She's just starting drama. It's some bullshit."

Our teacher looks up from his desk and says, "Gentlemen." Stern, serious. We start class, but my pulse never quite returns to normal.

I awkwardly don't turn in the sheet of problems that everyone else does. Camila eyes me again a few times during class and it's so, so strange that she's paying any kind of attention to me. I don't think I thought about her more than three times before last week. I doubt I took up too much of her brain space, either. But now she's on my mind every few minutes.

We really aren't supposed to have our phones out during the school day, and I usually am better about hiding it, but today I don't care. My phone is in my hand constantly. I turn off notifications for everything that isn't a text after getting one too many buzzes from my email account.

There isn't anything but the Joseph text until lunch,

when I finally get a text from Dad. I make my way to the little alcove where the back doors are to try and get away from the cafeteria noise. There aren't a ton of people passing by, but everything echoes around out here and it's overwhelming.

Rafael is safe, so is Jaslena. They're getting out of that situation. I don't know much else. I'm not sure how they're deciding to move forward but they're both safe right now.

I breathe out a little and try to relax. That's good, right? They're getting out. What does that mean?

I don't put my phone away. I stare at it and then I scroll through old texts between Rafael and me. Strings of emojis and all-caps messages. Our past conversations are the only way I can communicate with him right now. Was this something he was scared of? Having to deal with police and courts and Kyle? Like, officially deal with Kyle.

I wish he was here now, and I wish I could understand what this all means to him and his mom. He's not here, though. No one is. I open the message from Joseph.

Yo.

That's it. What the hell am I supposed to do with that? One word. Two letters. He can make me feel like total shit with two letters. I don't get it. I really don't. And I especially don't get why I text him back.

Hey :)

My legs feel kind of wobbly and I realize I haven't actually eaten yet today. From where I'm standing, tucked away against the back doors, I can hear all the chattering and joking around coming from the cafeteria. I'm not going in there. No way.

I just kind of wander the halls for the rest of the

period. When Joseph texts me again, I make myself look at the message right away.

You're in a better fucking mood I guess.

I don't know why, but it makes me cry.

The hallways are empty, for the most part. But just like the alcove, everything kind of echoes in the emptiness. Every sniff or choked-on breath feels amplified and exposed and I just want everyone to come back so I can hide among them all.

Before that happens, though, I wipe my face dry with the back of my wrist. I block Joseph's number, which feels impulsive and maybe kind of stupid, but I think of Rafael. And I think about what he said.

No one has a reason to hurt anyone, right? Right?

Maybe Joseph isn't hurting me. Maybe I was hurting myself with all of it. All of whatever is in my head.

So a boy kissed me.

So a boy wanted to do more than that.

I should care. I should like it. When I think about Joseph, I should feel more than empty. I should feel like I'm actually myself.

And I don't, and it just hurts.

So his number is deleted. Blocked. Whatever, that's fine. For a second, I feel good. For a second, I feel like I'm doing *something*, instead of ricocheting off the walls and corners of my mind like an echo with no place to go.

🎋 22 🎋

OKAY

WHEN I GET HOME from school, I feel ridiculously uneasy. Dad will actually be home for the night, which is good, but he's not here yet. Having Joseph's number blocked is making me more nervous than anything else. What if he's getting mad at me? What if he's telling me he's going to come over and I'm just not getting any kind of warning? I'm only keeping myself in the dark.

I should unblock him. I should. Should I?

I don't. I just go down to the lake to distract myself and look for the monster, which I'm basically sure at this point that I made up. When I think about seeing her in the water, the memory feels unreal. She was gigantic and shimmery and had those pink eyes. And it felt too *other*. Looking at her felt peaceful and enrapturing and wild. It's that feeling that has me convinced I was dreaming or something. It was too strange, too amazing. That magical, weightless, secure feeling that made so much sense at the time now feels impossible. Seriously impossible.

So maybe I made the whole thing up. Maybe it was

just a dream. Just dramatic, like the boys at school said. But I'm down here looking anyway because I don't want to think about everything that's going on.

There's nothing out here, which is exactly what I expected. Nothing but green water reflecting green trees and a silver, clouded sky. I check my phone and there still isn't anything from Rafael. There is something from Mei.

Are you okay?

It feels kind of weird that she sent that, and I don't know how to respond without making her worry so I just don't. But I text the same thing to Rafael. *Are you okay?* I hope more than anything that he'll answer. Maybe that's what Mei is feeling. Maybe anyone who's ever texted or emailed or written or spoken the words *are you okay* was desperate for an answer. Why is it such a hard question to answer?

As I'm stepping back inside, I hear the sound of a car pulling through Lake View, crunching across gravel. When I turn around, I see my dad pulling up in front of our trailer.

Usually, I'd be glad that he's home. I mean, I am glad. But he's acting weird. Exhausted. When he sees me glancing towards the fridge, he almost winces, so I don't say anything about having dinner. I don't say anything about anything, actually.

Everything is kind of awful. We're watching *How I Met Your Mother* reruns and I don't think I can talk about anything. Not Rafael, not Mei, not Joseph. Not what Dad ate today. I can't do anything at all.

The blocked number is making me uneasy. I get up and go to my room and try to put my DVDs back in place, but I can't get it right. There isn't a *right*, really, but everything I do feels weird. Every order I put them in, every sound they make.

Joseph was here last night. Joseph was here last night.

I almost unblock his number. I almost do it.

I toss my phone across the room instead. It makes a louder sound than I thought it would. From the living room, my dad calls, "Callie?" and I panic for a second because I realize I'm crying again—I don't even know what I'm crying about—and I don't want him to notice. Half my DVDs are on the floor, half are on the shelf, and all of them are wrong. Maybe I'll just throw them away.

"Are you okay?"

Why do people keep asking me that? Am I okay? Who cares!

"Yeah!" It's just one word so I hope it sounds normal. I think I pull it off, until I hear the squeaking of the couch and my dad getting up from it. I think he's coming over here.

"Callie?" He's in the doorway. I don't look at him. I think this looks bad. I think he thinks I'm going crazy. I think I can't get these DVDs just right and it's killing me a bit.

"I don't want to talk right now."

"Callie—"

"Please. Seriously, just please leave me alone."

"Callie, no. No, come on." Dad is shuffling into the room, and he knows I'm crying and being crazy and he doesn't know why, and really, I don't think I know either. "You don't have to talk to me, but you cannot be alone right now. Callie. Come on, bug. It's okay. It's okay."

For some reason, I'm sobbing into my dad's shoulder like I'm two years old, and for some reason, I don't care at all. For some reason, this is the only place I can stand to be. In the middle of a bunch of DVDs with some infomercial playing from the living room and my dad rubbing my back.

I can't explain anything to him. I think I lost my best friend and I think Rafael hates me and I think Joseph... I don't know what I think about him. Just that I think about him a lot and it always makes me nervous. I think my dad is slowly killing himself and I am too ridiculous to know what to do about it.

I think all of this and I think there's nothing I can do but cry and try not to notice that even with his arms around me, telling me everything's okay, I can feel my dad shaking. I can feel that everything is not.

23

STILL DO

I ALMOST DON'T GO to school the next day. I almost stay in bed instead. And, as I creep achingly through my classes, I figure it wouldn't have made much of a difference. I'm just a body walking around. I don't take anything in or realize anything around me. Until I see Camila Flores.

She's talking to Émilie, who I hardly know anything about. Before everything went down between her and Mei, Émilie was the only thing I even knew about Camila. They're the friends everyone knows. Camila and Émilie. Émilie and Camila.

They're talking at the corner of the science hallway while everyone switches classes around them, and they look so engaged. It's the first time I've seen Camila look anything but cool. Right now, talking to Émilie, she looks kind of goofy, kind of intense, kind of wild.

She's talking with big hand motions and laughing through her sentences while Émilie intently listens and laughs along. They're so very *together*. So very easy. And it's mesmerizing. It's like looking at the lake monster. Getting lost in something. The way they're talking together? It's safe. It's honest.

When Camila catches me staring (because I am staring, kind of ridiculously) her whole demeanor shifts to something a bit more neutral. Friendly but neutral. Not really her, not really whole. At least not next to the way she was before she caught me watching. She waves at me, and then Émilie notices I'm there and smiles my way even though we've never really talked.

I don't know why the two of them talking hit me like it did. I want to keep watching them but that's weird, and also, I don't know why I'd want to do something like that. Still, I guess I haven't moved for a while. I don't notice Mei coming up beside me.

"Hey!" She's so bright. So awake. I feel the opposite of awake.

"Do you know Émilie?" I ask her. And then I kind of remember that's not how conversations go. I haven't really talked to her for two days. "Hey. I mean, hi."

Mei smiles, but she's side-eyeing me with one eyebrow up, "Hey, girlie. I don't know her really, no. But her and Camila are, like, best friends."

"Yeah."

"We haven't talked in, like, a long time."

It takes me a second to realize she's talking about us and not Camila and Émilie. When I look at Mei, she's watching me, brows wrinkled. Concerned. I can feel the same expression on my face. "Twenty-four hours?" I ask. Testing. Prodding.

"A long time," Mei repeats. "Are you busy after school?"

No, I guess I'm not. But I can't really imagine hanging out with anyone. Even Mei, who is always really easy to hang out with.

"I, uh..." I don't know what to say because I kind of feel like I'm fading back into the nothingness of the day. Émilie and Camila have gone away, but the thought of them hanging out and laughing is the only thing that really keeps me from saying no. I'm not sure why. "Do you want to come over later?"

"Of course." Mei nudges me with her shoulder. "I've got dance until five, but I'll swing by after?"

"Okay. Oh, wait." I stop myself from leaving it at that. I push forward. I try. "Did you say anything to Camila? About prom? Are you going with her?" I'm not sure how I manage to get it all out. The question is so draining. And anyway, if Mei had decided to go with Camila, I'm pretty sure she would have told me.

"No." It's just one word but somehow, Mei manages to say it slowly. It's like she's testing the waters, just like me. Trying to see how I'll react, trying to figure out where we're at. Does she know I'm upset about this? I hope not. Oh God, I hope not. "Not yet."

"Do you know what you'll tell her?"

"I'm not sure." She says this slowly, too. And I feel like the worst friend because maybe she needs to talk about it with someone and I'm supposed to be the one she talks about this stuff with.

"You two would probably have a lot of fun together," I try. My voice sounds so ridiculously quiet.

"Yeah!" Mei sounds bright. Too bright. Which means she feels uncomfortable, which means I'm making her uncomfortable, which means that maybe she knows I have a crush on her. Maybe she doesn't want me to feel bad about it. Maybe she's not making any decisions about Camila because she's worried I'll be upset. Maybe, maybe, maybe.

"I'll see you later, then."

I start to walk away and this time I don't stop. I know I'm going kind of fast and being super weird, but I'm officially convinced that I'm making Mei feel like shit, which is possibly the worst feeling ever. Even worse than the fact that my instinct right now is to reach out to Joseph. To unblock his number and make up some reason why I haven't been responding to him and ask him, *is there any way I can make it right?* I hate it. I hate that that is what I feel like doing. Because I don't want to. Really, I don't. But for some reason, I feel like I should.

Too quickly, I zone out the entire rest of the hallway and when someone says, "Oh! Callie, hi!" I collide into their chest before I have a chance to register who it even is.

"Jian?" It's a big deal to not notice Jian. He's, like, a tree, height-wise. "Sorry." We stumble away from each other and then we're just staring. Wide eyes. Awkward people.

"Uh," I start. "Mei went that way."

"Oh." He looks down the hallway I'm pointing at. "No, yeah. I was actually... uh... I wanted to talk to you." He scratches at the back of his head and I think, yeah, Jian and I? We're probably feeling the same things right now. Out-of-place things, bad-at-casual-conversation things. Nerdy people things.

"Oh. What's up?"

"It's about Rafael, actually."

My heart speeds up. "Have you heard from him?"

"No. I was hoping you had."

"Ah..." I didn't think I could be more worried about everything with Rafael, but somehow, right now, I feel myself wanting more than ever to talk to him again. To apologize or just—I don't know. Hug him or something. "He hasn't said anything to me for a few days."

"Okay." And Jian looks... well, probably what I look like. His eyebrows are creased just slightly but just noticeably. He keeps fidgeting with his hair, his arms, his fingers. And when someone that tall gets fidgety, you really notice it.

"I'm sure..." What am I sure of? That he's okay? Maybe. Hopefully. But I don't know, not really. Yet seeing Jian like this, having an actual conversation with him for the first time maybe ever, it makes me want to believe everything is alright. For Jian. For me. For Raf. "I can let you know if I hear anything."

"Yeah. Okay... yeah, please do."

We stand there for a second, lockers screeching around us, classmates chattering and laughing and joking, and it's weird. I guess Jian and I might be weird. But it's nice when you see yourself in someone else. When you know you're not totally alone in whatever you're worrying about.

"Do I have your number?" I pull out my phone, knowing full well that I do not.

"Oh, uh, here." Jian takes my phone and taps in his information. When he hands it back, I stare at his name there on my screen. *Jian Huang*. Six years after meeting him, I can finally send him a text. So I do.

It's Callie :)

And he smiles at me. "I should, uh—" He points down the hall. "I've got Spanish."

"Yeah, yeah. I'll see you, Jian." He's starting to walk away, but before he can get too far, I call out, "Jian!"

He turns around.

Rafael would kill me for this. He really would.

But I think he'd smile about it too.

"I think Rafi really likes you."

I've never seen someone blush so hard, so fast. Jian's whole face goes red and his eyes dart around the hall like he's waiting for someone to say something about it.

"See you later." I wave. Jian and I have never talked much, but maybe we should. Maybe we will.

When I get home, I throw my phone under my bed somewhere so that I don't do anything stupid. With Dad still at work, I'm going to be alone for a bit, and I don't trust myself not to reach out to Joseph.

Mei won't be here for a while, and the thought of hanging out with her right now is making me antsy. I don't want to say anything stupid. I don't want to *feel* anything stupid. But I won't make this about me. Mei needs a friend. I'll figure it out. I'll be a friend. I'll make it work.

I wander down to the lake again, which feels even more pointless today than it did yesterday. I can't imagine seeing something like her—like the lake monster. I feel so out of it right now. It feels like nothing I've ever imagined has been real.

I haven't heard back from Rafael. I obviously don't have my phone right now, but I'm pretty sure I wouldn't find any new messages from him on there. I wonder how much he and Jian texted each other before everything that happened with Kyle. Maybe they were more serious than I realized. Nothing could have happened between them before that bonfire, right? But I guess I don't know. Rafael might not have told me. I hope that he would have. I want to ask him about it. I want to ask him about everything—Jian, and school, and what he wants to do after, and what happened after last night. God, I hate how things ended last night. My stomach sinks.

I need to give him space—I know I do—but as I'm walking away from the lake, I see Jaslena outside, heading towards the mailboxes, and I can't help but walk her way.

Behind her is a running car that I don't recognize. There's no one waiting in it, and she's got the keys dangling from her fingers. She's wearing pale green scrubs and her hair is knotted back into a frizzy bun.

When I say, "Hello," she looks startled, even though I've been coming her way for a while. Distracted, I guess. That makes sense.

"Callie! Hello!" She smiles and hugs me, but she looks so tired, like someone who just rolled out of bed.

"How are you?" I try to say it casually so she knows she doesn't have to talk about everything that happened. She pulls away and is still smiling. Still looking tired. There are wisps of her dark hair falling around her face and she pushes them back.

"Okay. We're okay."

I ask, "How's Rafael?" And want to ask more but stop myself.

"Oh, Callie, he will be okay. He's very strong."

I nod, because he is and because I think she's getting overwhelmed. Behind us, the car engine sputters on. This was clearly meant to be a quick stop. I want to ask if Rafael will be back in school, or ask where he is right now, but I don't.

Suddenly, I know what I should say—what I really *want* to say now—and it hits me unexpectedly, like the breeze that's coming off of Lost Lake. And I can't get the thought out of my head. I want to say it. Maybe it won't make sense. Maybe it will.

"I love you," I tell her. And it feels weird! But also... not. "You and Rafael? I love you two and I really hope—I just hope you're okay and everything works out."

Before I finish talking, Jaslena pulls me into a hug again, and I hug her back and wish everything could just be okay. Right now, for these few seconds at least, everything is.

I guess she kind of knows what I want to say because she just quietly tells me, "He'll talk to you when he's ready. He will."

I nod but don't say anything. When she pulls away, Jaslena tucks my hair behind one ear. She says, "You look like your mama, did you know that?" And I can't breathe for a second because: what? Why did she say that? I didn't expect to hear that. I wasn't prepared to hear it.

I know I look like my mom. I guess I just forget sometimes that other people knew her. I know my mom lived here for a while; I know that she and my dad planned to save money and move out. But then she got sick. And then it got hard. And then they got stuck. I know that. My dad doesn't talk about her, and I don't push him to. It's jarring whenever someone brings up how she existed in their lives, outside of my head.

And I guess in my head I know that people around here knew her. But it's strange for that to manifest itself. For my friend's mom to tell me I look like someone I never really met, that she knew better than I ever will.

I want to smile or something, but I honestly can't manage it. Jaslena hugs me again. I think she needs to not feel alone. I hope she's okay. At least, I hope that this is only a low point. That things get better. For Raf and for her.

"He'll talk to you when he can," she says when she pulls away.

"Okay," I say softly. She rubs my arm and smiles and says goodbye, and I'm standing by our mailboxes, wondering why anyone would treat someone like her badly.

I think I hate Kyle. I think Rafael was right about a million things but most of all this: that no one has a reason to hurt anyone. The thought is painful. It stings and sears, and I don't want to worry about it, but it's true.

No one has a reason to hurt anyone. But a lot of people still do.

24

KISS (I CAN'T FIND THE WORDS)

MEI COMES STRAIGHT to my house after dance, bangs pinned back, hair all messy, Nike sweatpants pulled over her pink leotard. She's always stunning, she really is. It's easy to remind myself why I didn't want to do this. Because she is Mei, and she is beautiful, and it's basically impossible not to think about that.

Neither of us have eaten all day and there isn't much food around the house, so we hike up the hill to Martin's to try and find something. It's a little bit of a good thing, because, even though I don't expect to see Rafael there, a part of me is hoping we'll run into him. That's sort of the only reason I'm not completely zoning out right now.

I don't want to say things are awkward between Mei and I, because that would actually kill me. But I've been acting intentionally distant and unintentionally weird, and Mei isn't stupid.

"You know," she says. We're nearly to the top of the hill and I am basically out of breath, but she somehow is not. "Jian wanted me to ask you if you've heard from Rafael."

"Really?"

"Yeah. I guess he hasn't been around school lately. He thought you might know something."

I wonder, again, if Rafael would have told Jian about Kyle. How close were they before everything got crazy? I still have no idea. Not knowing is killing me. I guess I could text Jian, since I actually have his number now.

"He's okay. I think. I guess I haven't seen him around much either." Not a lie. It's not really my place to tell Rafael's truth.

We make it to the door and the little bell dings as we walk in. The fluorescent lights are a bit alarming compared to how dark it was outside. It's still pretty early but there are more storm clouds coming in. No rain yet. It'll probably be crazy tonight.

I glance toward the register. No Rafael. Mei heads to the cooler and grabs a can of iced tea like she always does at places like this, and I follow her and get some coffee.

She comes up behind me and presses the cold drink against my arm and says, "Gotcha!" and genuinely, for a second, it makes me laugh, but I can't keep it up. I've got my coffee in hand and I can tell that Mei notices I'm being weird, and even before she says anything, I know we're going to talk about it. Right now, in Martin's All-Night Gas and Grub, we're going to talk about whatever dumb issues are going on between us.

I can tell that's what she wants to happen, even as she says, "Okay, Callie," and the lights flicker above us. I can see it in her eyes. Her smile dropped the second I stopped laughing, and now she's looking at me and saying, "What's going on?"

And I'm saying, "What?" even though that's a shitty and stupid thing to say. The idea of putting everything out there, of telling her everything, is kind of thrilling. Mostly terrifying, but a little bit thrilling. I get a little burst of adrenaline at the thought of it.

"You're acting weird," she says. And it's a powerful thing to say. Not everyone would try to talk about this. Not everyone would call out their friend for being passive-aggressive. And I usually love that about Mei— that she can face any issue head-on. But right now, it's making me jittery.

"Oh." And she's right. She's obviously right. "Yeah."

"Did I do something?" She crosses her arms and stands right across from me, and somehow looks so in control and so hurt at the same time. "Like... on the boat? Was that weird for you?"

"No!" Opposite. Opposite of weird. Why did she bring that up? What does she think happened on the boat? I think I'm actually shaking right now. I feel light-headed and dizzy.

"Then what the hell is going on? I can tell you're uncomfortable—"

"I'm not uncomfortable."

"You are. You never tell me this kind of thing."

"What?"

"Like if you're uncomfortable. I can tell when you are, but it's like you're afraid to say anything."

Afraid to say anything? I don't know. I guess. Maybe,

probably. Not with her, though. I don't know how she would have noticed.

I don't say anything, and she goes on. "Like at the bonfire. You didn't want to drink; I don't think you wanted to—to talk to Joseph." I wince. "But you didn't say anything."

"Okay, why does this—how can you tell?"

"I just know you, Callie. I know you get quiet when something bothers you, and I know you think no one gets it, whatever's going on. You think no one gets it. But I can tell when you're upset. I can tell you've been upset, and I don't get why. Did I do something?"

"You didn't do anything."

"Then what—"

There are a million things I could say. A million reasons why I've been acting so selfishly and weirdly. And I don't know why I don't tell her one of those; that I'm worried about my dad and I'm worried about Rafael and I'm scared to run into Joseph. I don't tell her that she's amazing and awesome and I want her to have fun and be happy. I don't tell her any of that. For some reason, in the Middle of Martin's, with a crazy storm threatening to burst outside and tears threatening to burst from her eyes, I tell Mei, "I'm asexual."

And she opens her mouth right away but doesn't say anything for a second. I don't think that's what she was really expecting to hear. Which is fair. It certainly wasn't what I was expecting to say. Mei uncrosses her arms and shifts on the balls of her feet and says, "You're—"

"Everybody get down!"

What?

Immediately, my heartbeat speeds up. I don't know who said it. Maybe Martin. Maybe a customer. Whoever it was sounded frantic. Something about their voice—urgent and different—instantly inspires panic. We're behind the coffee maker and I can't really see what's going on at the front of the store. For some reason, all I can picture is that drunk guy from a few nights ago. I lean to the right. Look. See. See it. I clamp a hand over my mouth to stop from screaming.

"Someone has a knife," I whisper to Mei. She almost goes to look but I pull her back towards me and crouch down. I'm holding her hand. Tightly. I'm not sure who else is in the store. I'm still not sure who yelled.

I am sure about the knife.

"What the hell, what the hell, what the hell." Mei keeps mouthing the words frantically and I pull her more towards me so that we're sort of hugging and sort of huddled as flat against the counter as possible.

There's talking. The guy with the knife must be talking. I hear the register open and then I hear someone yell, "Come on!" and then some kind of strangled sound.

I didn't see the guy. I saw the knife.

Mei is shaking and I think I might be too, but I'm too scared to say anything, so I just grab her other hand and try to get us closer together than we already are. Her eyes are squeezed shut.

He doesn't know we're here. He doesn't know we're here.

I'm not sure how long it takes. I'm not sure if anything else is said. There's roaring in my ears and I feel like I can't breathe. I press my forehead against Mei's and she opens her eyes and I lean back so I can see her better. I think we just sit like that, looking at each other, for an eternity. At some point, a little tear slides down her cheek and I wipe it out of the way.

The bell on the door rings. We don't move. There's a hand on my shoulder. I jump. I think I yell.

"It's okay!" When I look up, I see Martin. He's holding his hand out to me, so I take it and I get up and he keeps asking us, over and over, *are you okay? Are you girls okay?* He seems pretty shaken up, but he's called the police and Mei is still holding my hand and did that really just happen? Did it really?

I can't believe Rafael works here.

EVENTUALLY THE POLICE ARRIVE AND TRY TO TAKE statements. I don't have much to tell them. I don't have much to say. I didn't see a face. I heard a male voice. Mei didn't see anything. We were the only ones in the store besides Martin. We were together the whole time.

Mei calls her mom, who drives over here in less time than makes sense from her house. She hugs Mei, and she hugs me, and then she's talking to the police.

I try calling my dad, but he doesn't pick up. I even call Terry once, but she doesn't either. I text them both, tell them to call me. I don't really want to describe any of this over a text. I'm exhausted. Nothing happened to us. Nothing happened to anyone. But I feel like I'll pass out in a few seconds.

I see Mei sitting on the bench outside the store.

There's a police car next to her with its lights still flashing, but everyone else is inside. When I sit down, she shifts right up against me and I hug her. I want to laugh or cry or something, but I just say, "I'm so sorry!"

"You're not the one who robbed a gas station."

"I know, but I'm really sorry, Mei." And I don't know why, but I am kind of laughing and kind of crying. In any other scenario, this would be wildly crazy-looking, but right now, I think the both of us are too hyped up on adrenaline. We've got too much stuff coursing through our veins. I've got my arms wrapped around Mei still and her shoulders are shaking. When she looks at me, I can tell she's kind of laugh-crying too and it makes me love her so, so much.

I know that sounds crazy.

Maybe I'm crazy.

There are teardrops caught in her eyelashes and she's biting her bottom lip and she's such a beautiful person.

"I like you." I just say it. "Like. Mei. I really like you."

"You mean—"

"I mean like a crush. This timing is so shitty, wow!" I let go of her and run both of my hands through my hair—it's all tangled and probably looks ridiculous. There are police in the building behind us investigating a robbery we were present for. Less than an hour ago, I couldn't even talk to Mei. And now I'm sitting here, and I think we're both exhausted, and it looks like it'll start raining any second.

"Hey." Mei takes my wrist and holds my hand, and she looks confused, so confused, but also not mad. Maybe kind of intrigued.

"I like you." I say it again, because for some reason, I feel like I can. Her hand is warm in mine, even though it's starting to feel a little cold out here. "You're my favorite person and I miss you when we don't talk, even if it's just for twenty-four hours." That makes her laugh. It's a breathy kind of thing and my heart feels so full. I say, "But you're my friend. And I want you to be happy. Okay? Seriously, seriously happy. And if Camila makes you happy—"

"*You* make me happy."

That takes my breath away. Really, I'm not breathing. And I'm inexplicably reminded of seeing the lake monster. It's that feeling. Yesterday, I was sure it wasn't real, but right now, looking at Mei, I'm so sure it's the realest feeling there is. Wild and magic and *possible*. Everything feels possible.

It's some kind of love. It's easy.

"I don't... all that stuff with Camila." Mei looks at me and I have no idea what she's thinking. I just know that it'll be fine. Whatever it is, her and I will be fine. I think, in the end, we always will be. "Callie, I like you. I think I have for a seriously long time. I think you snuck up on me. I've known you for so long."

"Too long?"

"Never too long."

I breathe in. I breathe out. Mei says, "But in there. In there you said—you're asexual?"

I don't know why I was scared of this conversation before. At least, having this conversation with Mei. I nod.

She smiles and she says, "Okay. What does it mean? For you, I mean. I know it's different for everyone. What does that mean for you?"

I don't really know how to find the words for it. I just know that I don't want to look away from Mei right now. I know that I could be with her for hours and hold her hand until the end of time. Cheesy. Romantic. I know. Who cares!

I lean towards her slowly, even though we're already kind of close. "Can I..."

Mei is staring at my lips. She is. And she nods, just slightly, so I do it.

I kiss her. I kiss her and the little breath she takes when our lips touch is like heaven. She kisses me. We're kissing. And it's good.

But when Mei's eyes open, and I see her face, and the expression on it—kind of dreamy, kind of smiling; eyelids low, blinking softly—that's even better.

I will eventually find the words to tell her all of this. To explain it in a way that makes sense. That kissing her makes me happy, because I'm pretty sure it makes *her* happy. I'm still figuring it out, I really am, but there are some parts of myself that are very simple and very clear.

Maybe I don't care so much about kissing, but I care a lot about Mei.

"Was that crazy?" I ask her. She nods.

"The good kind, though."

"Okay." We're talking softly. Like we did that night on the boat. I laugh. "Okay. Yeah."

Mei wraps her arms around my shoulders and when she laughs, I feel it on my neck.

If this is love, love is easy.

Mei and Callie. Callie and Mei.

Wild. Magic. Possible.

25

I GET SOME NEWS

FOR A SECOND, everything is perfect. Yes. Perfect. For at least a second, I swear it is.

We have to go; of course we do. Mrs. Huang is still shaken up (I probably am too, but all I can think about is *Mei*) and she tells me to call her if I don't hear back from Dad soon.

There are smatterings of raindrops coming down now. Nothing crazy, but it feels like something more is on the way. Before Mei leaves, she wraps me in a hug and says, "I'll call you."

All I can think is how much that sounds like some suave line from some suave movie, and it almost makes me laugh, except Mrs. Huang is watching us and I think if I laughed right now, she might actually pass out.

"Okay."

I'm absolutely buzzing. As soon as they're gone, I head out to the lake.

I know it's going to rain, I know I should probably try harder to get in contact with my dad, but I have to be out there on the water. Realistically, I'm fine. Realistically, he probably saw the missed calls and figured I was trying to check in on him again. Realistically, I shouldn't think there's a lake monster in my backyard, but right now, I've never been more sure that she's out there.

I run out to the dock, to the boat, to the water. I'm kind of shaky—the adrenaline, the everything—but I manage to get the boat turned over and in the water. I'm hopping in as I'm pushing off the shore. It's an all-in-one kind of motion. I'm full of something I don't understand. The rain is coming a bit steadier now. It's making small noises as it connects with the water. Little droplets are getting stuck in my hair.

"You're using my boat?" I hear Mr. Jones' voice before I'm even three yards out on the lake.

"Is that okay?" Normally, this conversation would freak me out. Mr. Jones is way too wise and cool to not be intimidating. But I'm running on fumes, or magic, or the sip of gas station coffee I managed to steal before everything got crazy. "Rafael said it'd be okay."

"It's okay." He's standing there on his back porch, looking kind of grumpy in a bathrobe and slippers. "Yeah, it's fine."

"Okay," I say. "Thank you."

"It's gonna rain."

"I'll be careful." Easily the longest conversation I've ever had with him, and definitely the boldest. As I paddle away, Mr. Jones watches for a bit before waving a hand my direction and stomping back inside. I think grumpy people might just be lonely. I think I'm going to find my monster.

I feel like I did when I first saw her—I feel like nothing matters. Or maybe everything does. Out here, there's no such thing as eating disorders, or abuse, or loss, or pain. There's no such thing as Joseph DeLarino or plastic cases of DVDs. There's just this: the water and the possibility of something strange below it. Something wild and safe and overwhelming.

I watch. I squint. I look.

I'm sure I'll see something. I'm sure.

I keep paddling, farther out than I've ever been before. Past Lake View and the forests and the trees, all the way to the nicer houses with their private docks and landscaped yards. I keep going, keep looking and watching, and I feel it. That... whatever it was, the first time I saw the monster. It's safe out here—even though it might storm. It's wild out here—even though I'm just me. Just Callie Catwell.

I don't see anything until I see her. Not the monster. Not yet. But there's a woman, or the outline of one, sitting on the end of a long, old dock. And it takes me a second to remember where I am, to remember why, as I paddle closer to it, this dock makes me nervous. It's longer than the others. It seems strangely unkempt. The woman is as far out over the water as you can be without falling in, feet swinging idly back and forth.

Rafael and I passed by this house on the way to the inlet fire. We heard yelling. We walked away.

But here is this woman. She is more than an outline now. She is a person. And she is familiar. I didn't even realize I had been navigating in her direction. She doesn't seem to notice me, even though she's watching Lost Lake very intently.

"Oh." I can't help saying it. The woman looks over to me slowly, calmly. It's eerie out here—not in a bad way—with the clouds crowding over us and the dark water reflecting them. And the woman, looking at me, blinking slowly. "You were on TV."

She laughs—a gentle thing.

Of course, she was on TV. She's the woman from the channel eight news reports—the woman who saw the lake monster. The woman from the yelling house. The woman on the dock. The woman who no one believed.

I ask her, "Are you looking for the monster?"

"I suppose. Are you?"

"Yes."

"Have you seen her before?"

"Yes."

"I'm sorry that you had to."

I don't know what that means. I think about the time I saw the monster. It wasn't long ago. I was worried about something. About a million things. I was worried. I was scared. And then there she was.

I want to ask the woman about the first time she saw the monster. I want to ask her what it was like. I want to ask her about the man she lives with in that house and if he yells a lot. I want to ask her thousands of things.

But then I hear tires on pavement and the rumbling of an opening garage. The woman looks back towards her house and she looks different. She looks alert and exhausted all at once. High shoulders, drooping eyes.

When she stands up, I am worried for her. I am worried that no one believed her. I am worried.

"That monster," the woman says. Her voice is quiet but strong. A whisper that I cannot miss. "She's looking out for us."

And then she's gone. Back to her house. Back to that man.

In the lake, I see nothing.

Everything comes back. This is the problem with being dramatic. This is the problem with needing to talk but having no one to talk to. Everything I do is impulsive. Everything I do is chaotic. I jump to conclusions before I have time to process a single thing that is going on.

I kissed Mei.

I *kissed* Mei.

What the hell? Why would I do that? And why would I assume that a kiss would change anything between us for the better? Would she want to do other things? Besides kissing? Would I want to? No. No, no, no.

My heart is beating. I can feel it beating. You can't always feel it beating, can you?

For a moment there, I thought everything was okay. Well. Maybe not. Maybe I just wasn't thinking at all. At least, I wasn't thinking enough.

Focus on the good things. That's bad advice. I focused on the good things and I forgot the stupid ones. I forgot that I don't actually know where my dad is right now, and I forgot that Rafael hasn't talked to me in days. I forgot that telling someone you like them implies certain things. And there are definitely things I don't want it to imply.

Mei will understand, right? Mei will get it, she'll listen.

Maybe she won't.

Joseph never did.

But I can't blame him, can I? I never tried to tell him what I was feeling. I never tried to tell him to stop, did I? Shit. I've been ignoring him, too. What's going to happen when we run into each other? Because, eventually, we will. Lost Lake is a small town. What the hell am I supposed to say? I can't be mad at him. I can't be scared of him. I have no right. I have no right. He didn't hurt me. I have no right.

It's raining. Of course it's raining. The sky has been waiting to rain all day. Now, the drops are coming down. Giant and glassy and quick. Quicker. Speeding up.

There is nothing in the water. There is just me, on a boat, panicked and alone.

When my phone starts buzzing, I almost jump into the murky lake. I'm getting a call. A call from Terry.

I answer right away.

"Hello?" I'm worried.

"Callie?" It's her. It's Terry from work. Her voice is deeper than I expected. Richer. I can't tell the tone yet. But she's never called me before, so I'm assuming something strange is going on.

"Yeah. Yeah, this is Callie. Hi." She's probably just replying to my phone call. I've never called her before either and I don't often call my dad when I know he's at work. This is just about my phone calls. This is just about that.

"Hi, sweetie. This is Terry. Callie, um. Oh honey. Something's happened to Michael. He's—your dad, I mean—"

"What?"

Terry takes a breath on the other end and I think she's trying to calm down, but even through the phone line, I can hear the way it wobbles and catches in her throat.

"Something happened today at work. Your dad—he's in the hospital."

26

THE MONSTER

I'M ROWING to the shore as fast as I can. I'm beyond being aware of my own body. Breathing, panting, choking on air and rain and the hair that's falling into my face; it's all happening around me. Not to me. The rain is coming down in sheets now. I can't see three feet in front of me. It's all just water, gray bullets falling from the sky.

My dad is in the hospital. He's in the hospital. Again.

"Fuck." I hate the sound of my voice. It's all strangled and crazy. What did Terry say? She's coming to pick me up? Yes. Right. She'll be here as soon as she can. She's coming to pick me up.

Dad is in the hospital.

For a panicked moment, I'm sure I've been steering myself in the wrong direction. How far out was I really? I feel like I've been working at the oars for hours. I need to get out of the water right now. But then I see the concrete launch point come into view, and the old dock, a murky point in the distance.

There's someone right at the water's edge.

Rafael?

I've got no reason to believe it's him. I *want* to believe it's him. I paddle faster. Through the rain, the figure starts to become clearer. But it's raining too hard, I can't be sure. I think it's Rafael, I think it's him.

It's Joseph.

I can't believe this is happening right now. It's different than before. It's different from all the other times I've been around him. For some reason, I need to stay away from him. Everything in me says to stay away, to stay out on the water. He can't get me on the water.

Get me. What does that even mean? I've got no reason to be scared. Not really. I feel scared, though. More than I usually am.

Joseph is at the docks. I'm sure that it's him. I've stopped rowing but I can tell. The lanky way he's hunched over, very still, even in the rain. Menacing.

I hate storms, I really do.

I don't know what to do. I have to get out of the boat to get to Terry and my dad. But that's where Joseph is. I think he's saying something. I can't hear over the roaring rain.

Thunder cracks and I flinch, and I know I can't stay out on the water.

Shit, shit, shit.

I row to the shore. Towards Lake View Mobile Home Park, even though I can't see any of the trailers through the rain. All I can see is Joseph. It all feels wrong. There is no good option here. If I stay, I don't get to Dad. If I go, I'm going right to Joseph.

"Catwell, what the fuck!" He's yelling. Not to be heard over the rain. Just to yell.

I'm getting closer to him and it feels wrong. Mr. Jones's boat scrapes against the cement incline.

"What are you doing here?" I'm sure he can't hear me through the rain. There's a giant cracking sound. Lightning shrieks across the sky. Joseph is in the water, tugging the boat closer to the launch point.

"Come on, get out of there." He doesn't sound kind. He doesn't sound like he's concerned for my safety. Joseph just sounds angry. He always just sounds angry. "Hurry the fuck up, Callie."

I scramble out of the boat, stumbling into the shallow water. The cement is slick with algae and I almost fall. Joseph catches my arm. I'm not in the water, but he's grabbing me, tugging me away. Too hard, too fast. I slip again. He's got both my arms. He's not letting go.

"The hell is your problem, Catwell?"

I don't know what he's talking about. The boat isn't secured. It's floating and drifting vaguely behind us. We're both soaked. All I can see is him. All I can see is Joseph. The boat is floating away. If Terry gets here, I won't be able to see her. The rain is too heavy, too loud. Joseph shakes my arms.

He roars, "Callie!"

"Let go."

He doesn't. He might not have heard me.

"Joseph, let go."

"You know, you're really testing me. I come all the way out here—"

"I didn't ask you to come."

"Even though you haven't responded to me for days—"

"Joseph, let go!"

"I save your stupid ass. And you're mad at me?"

"I'm not mad at you." Maybe I am. Maybe I always have been. Joseph's hands are wrapped around my arms still. His touch is cold, like something dead and dark. The shadows over his eyes are like coffins. Coffins for cold, dead eyes. I pull away. He pulls back.

"Hey, hey, don't be like that." Joseph steps close to me and his voice is different. His mouth is right against my ear. "We can still make this work."

He is so, so close to me. Right up against me, completely against me. One of his hands moves to my waist. But he's grabbing me and it's painful. I stumble away. I yank myself away from him.

"No."

"The fuck—"

"No. I don't want to do this." My feet splash in the rising water. There is no one around. There is nowhere to go that he couldn't follow me to. "Go away. Just leave me alone. I don't want to make this work. No!" He steps closer to me and I almost fall trying to get away.

The rain is everywhere. It is all that there is. The rain and me and Joseph. Me and Joseph and the incessant, relentless rain.

There's water in my eyes and I can't keep track of Joseph or the dock or the boat or anything. I feel his hand grab at my wrist again and when I try to pull away, he just pulls me closer to him. Against him. Against him. Against him.

I want to scream. I want to yell. There is no one

around. I want to fight. But all I can do is breathe. When I open my mouth, only stupid, useless air comes out and mingles with the storm and I am panicking. Because all I can do is breathe. Any scream gets swallowed into my lungs and makes my heart beat a thousand times faster.

This is it.

I stumble backwards and this time, I fall onto the ground.

This is happening.

And Joseph stumbles on top of me. His legs pinning down my legs. My legs trapped by the slick concrete.

This is happening. It's happening

"Stop." I'm choking on air and water, and I'm sure he doesn't hear me. He must not hear me. "Stop."

I don't have the resources inside me to cry. I have nothing. He has it all.

"You're okay," he tells me. "You're okay."

I am not. I do not move. I do not think that I can. I feel the rain. I feel him. There is nothing else.

Concrete and me and Joseph and the storm.

This was always going to be it, wasn't it? This is what Rafael meant. This is what he saw. He saw a person who doesn't mind hurting other people. He saw someone like Kyle. No one has a reason to hurt anyone, but Joseph is the kind of person that will hurt someone anyway.

The storm and Joseph and me and concrete.

But then he's gone. He's not here. There's a thump, a grunt. At first, I don't know why. My eyes are closed. I don't remember closing them. But I open them, and I see it. I see her—the lake monster. Silvery, and wild, and real.

She's perched on the launch point—sitting over me—

huge body and rose-colored eyes looking down on Joseph. He is on the ground, away from me, half in the water. On his back. She knocked him away. She roars. It's louder than the rain, louder than anything that is going on. The sound reverberates inside of me and I cannot get up, but I am not scared. Joseph is scared. He's trying to stand, trying to get away.

There is a monster roaring over me.

She ducks towards him, once, and he scuttles in the opposite direction. Away from her, away from the water, away from me.

Away from me. He is getting away from me. And the rain is still here. It is still falling but not as harshly or cruelly as before. There is a monster next to me, looking at me, watching me. And Joseph is running away.

I sit up from the concrete and start to feel like one person again. I can feel the scrapes on my elbows and the tears in my clothes and skin and when I look at her, the monster leans down, nudging my foot. Her eyes are wide, gigantic, and so rosy pink. I cannot imagine her, even as I'm watching her.

I stand up. She shimmies a little farther into the water. I follow her to the edge.

She makes a noise—a soft, gentle thing—then blinks, turns away, and dives back into the green, strange water of Lost Lake, making ripples against the rain drops, and I know that it was all real. All of it.

Mr. Jones's green rowboat bumps into the concrete at my feet and I blink. I am not myself. Or I am, more than I ever have been.

I pull the boat to shore; I stow it in the long grass.

When Terry arrives, the rain is just a shadow of the storm, and I climb into her car, soaked and battered and strange, and I cannot say a word.

27

I CAN ONLY DO ONE THING

TERRY DOESN'T SAY anything when I get in the car. She looks at me, mustering a watery smile, and tucks my hair behind my ears like Rafael's mom did earlier today. Earlier today was so long ago.

"Oh no." She points to my shoulder. I guess it's bleeding. "What happened there?"

"I fell." I'm bleeding everywhere; my knees are scraped up and my elbows are stinging. "Your seats."

"Hon, I don't care about the car. Are you okay? What happened? You're all scuffed up."

I nod, which isn't really an answer. What else can I do? I'm nervous about my dad, but distantly, I am also caught up in something else. My feet are up on the seat and my arms are around my legs and I feel so small. I think I must be fine. Because I put the boat back. Because it wasn't as bad as it could have been.

"Sweetie." Terry looks my way, but I don't really register it. "It seems like he's going to be okay. That's what they were tellin' me. He'll be okay. Just needs a bit of recovery time. All right?"

"Okay."

"Are you all right?"

I almost tell her, but I don't know *what* I would tell her. I'm just me. What is there to tell? I know Terry. She's Terry from work. But I guess I don't know her really. I don't know anyone.

I don't know how long it takes us to get to the hospital. I don't think about anything until we're there. And then we're inside, and it's so cold and my clothes are all wet, and I wish I could take them off and throw them into a fire. Someone is leading us down a hallway that is very white and sterile and lit up.

And then I'm seeing my dad in a white, sterile, lit-up bed and I'm suddenly choking on air. I suddenly cannot breathe at all. There is my dad. Here is me. Here I am. Terry is rubbing my back, I think, and she's sitting me down in a chair and my dad is saying, "Callie, Callie, Callie." And I don't even know where I am, not really. Not really.

"Callie."

"Dad."

"It's okay."

"No." It's not. He's in the hospital. He looks half dead. I am half dead. I've got no reason to feel like that. Terry is gone. No. She said she'd wait outside. She's here. She's with us. She's giving us a minute.

My dad is holding my hand tight, and I am crying and so is he.

"Callie. I'm sorry."

"I'm sorry."

I'm sobbing into the mattress and Dad's hand is on my back, and I can't tell him why I'm upset. I don't know why I am.

And also, I do.

I am so, so lost. I do not know anything at all, and that is possibly the only thing I know for sure.

⚜

I WAKE UP. I DON'T KNOW WHEN I FELL ASLEEP. I'M leaning over the hospital bed, and Dad has fallen asleep, too. My head is resting on my arms and I'm looking at him and I wonder when it started getting really bad again. Because if I think back to a few months ago, he didn't look like this. He didn't look pale and stretched and hurting. When did it start to change? It had to have been before he picked up all those extra shifts, but I really don't know if I noticed.

You never notice changes when they're gradual and tricky enough. Like going from healthy to sick. From friends to soulmates. From broken up to hanging out again to getting hurt.

I still think I let it happen. But now I'm thinking maybe I'm wrong about that, at least.

"Callie?" Dad. His eyes are just hardly open. I sit up quickly and it makes my head hurt. "What happened to you?"

At first, I think that's a crazy question for him to be asking me from *his* hospital bed, but then I remember I'm all scuffed up. I don't know how long I've been here, but my hair and clothes still feel damp. The rain is still on me.

"You first?" I say. My voice is scratchy, like I've been yelling for hours.

Dad sighs. His hand is resting on my arm, and he rubs his thumb back and forth. He's looking at the top corner of the opposite side of the room. Then he looks at me and his thumb stops moving and he kind of nods, kind of bobs his head a few times and says, "There were too many bad days, I suppose."

"Did you... What happened?"

"I was getting coffee for Terry," he says. His voice is very deliberate and very honest. I guess I can always tell when he's being honest. That sounds stupid, but it's comforting. He is real. He is a fact.

We are not just stories and legends.

Or maybe we are. Maybe everything is. But legends can be real too. Legends can tell the truth. Legends can tell about life.

Dad says, "And I collapsed before I made it out of the break room. Callie," he looks at me. I mean, he already was. Rather, he looks at me more intensely, his brows frowning a bit. "I am sorry."

"You don't have to be sorry," I whisper.

"I shouldn't have started working more," he says. "It was a bad idea. I don't manage all... *this*. I don't manage it well."

I bob my head up and down like he was doing before, and I realize he was probably doing it to keep himself from crying. That's why I'm doing it anyway.

"We don't talk about these things. *I* don't talk about

these things with you, and I should. All of it. The working —I was thinking about college for you."

That kind of gets me. "We've never even talked about that."

"Yeah. Yeah. We need to."

"I haven't even thought about college."

"That's okay. That's okay. I wanted to save up some more. In case you ended up wanting to go to school. I thought I was looking out for you."

I really had no idea. Dad was trying to afford tuition?

"And all of this..." Dad looks around the hospital room, all the clean whiteness of it. There's gentle rustling in the hallways and fluorescent lights flickering on outside the window. This isn't where we wanted to be. Not again. "You have eyes like your mom."

"Mom?" My heart stutters. I don't think Dad has ever brought her up. He's never initiated any conversations about her. There's a tear running down his right cheek, all the way to his chin.

"It got out of hand. When your mom died... I didn't know how to deal with anything, Callie. But I needed to be there for you. I wanted to make sure you had a good life."

"It is good." I'm crying again. More than Dad. He wipes some of my tears away with his thumb.

"It was hard to keep everything going. It was just easy to not worry about cooking and eating and... oh, it got out of hand... I don't want it to get like this again. This isn't something that needs to happen again. You and Terry... I think I'm the luckiest man in the world to have you two in my life. But I don't want it to come to this again."

And I know that it might. That we might find ourselves back in the hospital at some point. That the bad days could spiral into something worse. But it's okay. We'll try—together—to figure it out. Together. I think with this kind of thing—eating disorders and family members that I will never have the chance to meet—*together* is key.

"Okay." My dad sniffs, and, all right, maybe he was crying just as bad as me. I think we're both a mess. Obviously. Obviously, obviously. I wonder if Terry is still around here somewhere. Dad says, "What happened to you?"

My heart sinks. I think for a second I had forgotten. Or at least, it wasn't consciously on my mind. The rain, the storm, Joseph.

Joseph.

Joseph.

Joseph.

It's like he's back and I don't know what to say.

"Callie. What's wrong?"

"Joseph..." I breathe a too-deep, too-sudden breath. Every way that I could continue this sentence feels wrong. Every word feels wrong. I don't let them get to my tongue.

Attacked me.

Assaulted me.

Wrong, wrong, wrong. I am wrong. I must be.

I don't want to say anything, but then my phone buzzes in my pocket—I can't believe it's still there and functioning after the rain—and I don't check it but I have this hope, like I've had all week, that it's Rafael texting me. Letting me know how he is. Where he is. What he's doing.

All I'm thinking about is Rafael. About that night where he came to our door, and he was bleeding, and he said that no one has a reason to hurt anyone. Not Kyle or Joseph or anyone. They don't have a right to us. Joseph doesn't have a right to *me*.

"I think—" No, I don't think. I know.

Everything hurts. I think of the monster—my monster. And the woman on the dock. And Mei. I think of strong things. I try to be one.

"Joseph tried to have sex with me. Outside. By the lake." Joseph was wrong.

My dad doesn't say anything. I can feel the way neither of us are breathing. Everything hurts so, so badly.

"I told him 'no'." And I did this time. Out loud this time. I said *no*. I'd been saying it for weeks. Not out loud, maybe. But I never said *yes* out loud either. I never said yes to anything. To being in a relationship, to touching in the hallways, to kissing in my room. I never said yes. I never did. "I told him 'no' but he still tried to—he still tried to—"

That's it. That's it. I'm breathing and it's all I'm doing and I'm doing it wrong. Too fast. Too fast. Not me. I'm not me. And I am. I am a fact. I am a legend.

I am a strong thing, even when I break.

I told Dad. I said it. So this is real and this all happened and I am officially saying that Joseph was wrong. Is wrong. He is wrong. I am saying it and it hurts; so, so badly, it hurts.

He was wrong. I was not. That is a fact, even if I can't internalize it right now.

"*Dad.*" Strangled. I can't breathe. He's the one in the hospital, but I can't breathe. I think I'm going to die. I think maybe I am. There are things happening around me. Maybe there are. I don't feel them or notice them. There are more people, there is talking, there is Terry and Dad and some doctors, and I am breathing. That is all I can do. I can only do one thing. Anything else is too much.

I can only do one thing. I can only breathe.

It'll all go back to normal, I guess. Normal will be different, but it'll all be normal eventually. We'll find a routine. We'll figure it out.

I don't like making people out to be bad—people I know. I don't like it. But some people are bad, I guess. Some people are bad, I know.

It'll go back to normal. It'll go back to normal. A form of normal that comes after the old one gets shattered.

And that's good. The old normal was getting scary and toxic and bad. People weren't eating, people weren't good, I was not honest.

I'm going to be honest now. I'm going to try to be honest.

❧ 28 ❧

UNKNOWN NUMBER 9:27 PM

9:27 PM
Hey is this your number Callie?
This is Camila.
Flores.
Rafael gave me your number.

10:58 PM
Okay maybe he gave me the wrong one but in case he didn't: um, I'm not mad at you? Or anything like that! If you thought I was mad, I'm not mad! If you didn't think that, I'm sorry I just made you think it.

I just wanted to say that Mei talked about you a lot, and I'm glad you two are a thing and I think you're going to prom together? Which is cool.

11:15 PM
Okay. I don't think you're getting these.

But if you are, I'm sorry if I made things weird between you two. Tbh I kind of thought you were dating Joe DeLarino? Glad you're not. He's a dick.

11:21 PM

I don't know if this is relevant at all but I kind of had a huge crush on my friend Émilie last year. It was, like, right after I came out. And it was the worst because she's my best friend, right? And she didn't feel the same way. And that was just, wow, so hard for a while. Because, best friends, you know?

They're worth the world.

Anyway. It didn't work out between Émilie and I, but I guess it did with you and Mei, which is awesome.

11:29 PM

If that reads bitter I didn't mean for it to.

Émilie and I are cool now, by the way. I guess it did work out between us. Which is awesome.

12:01 AM

Anyways, just realizing I sent you a ton of stuff and we've never really even talked so that's weird. Kinda hoping you don't get all these!! Ha.

But I'm not mad at you, or anything like that. I'm happy. Seriously happy.

29

THIS ALL ENDS SO WE CAN START
SOMETHING NEW

I GUESS BEING best friends with the person you have feelings for is kind of crazy. Kind of in the bad way, sometimes in the good way.

We're sitting with Camila and Émilie at prom tonight? Also, Mei asked me to prom?

She did it while we were watching an Artsy Kid movie. The main characters were all ditching the dance to go hang out at some dingy all-night diner. Mei grabbed my hand and said, "Do you wanna not ditch prom with me?"

And I just looked at her and couldn't talk for a second and my mouth was hanging open, and I said, "Um. Obviously."

So here I am. In the living room, wearing some floor-length gown Terry helped me find at a thrift store last week. It's orange. I can't believe my life. Really, I can't believe it.

"I like it," Dad says. "Do you like it? You should. You look amazing."

"Okay." I wave a hand at him.

"None of that," he says, kind of serious. He started going to therapy again, so things are very much no-useless-negativity around here.

I'm supposed to start going to therapy next week, too. I'm nervous. I don't always think my problems are the kind of problems that warrant someone else worrying about. But maybe that's the point. I'm trying not to think about it too much tonight.

Tonight is prom. Tonight is the night every Artsy Kid dreads. Unlike the Artsy Kids, I'm kind of excited.

"I'm just nervous." Which is true. I've never been to a dance with someone I actually cared about going to a dance with. The stakes are higher, I guess. But every time I take a second and actually think about it—Mei and I, hanging out, listening to music—I relax. Because that's what this is.

Us.

Mei and Callie. Callie and Mei.

Dad has been pretty relaxed about the two of us. I think after everything that went down with Joseph, anything would be relaxing.

Joseph.

I'm not scared of him. Not like I used to be. I didn't realize that's what it was: fear. Thinking about him kind of makes my stomach hurt, but not in the scared way anymore. I don't like that he was okay with doing what he did. It's that simple and that strange. I don't like it.

But I'm not worried about running into him at the dance or anything like that. Joseph never cared about that kind of stuff.

Plus, I think he's been avoiding me.

Joseph. Avoiding me. A week ago, the idea of it wouldn't have made any sense.

I don't really know what happened there, with the monster. With him. But I think he's scared of me now. In the same way he's always been scared of Mei. Weird power. Silent power. Wild power.

I'll take it.

I think that if there is magic in Lost Lake—or weird science, or strange phenomenon of the natural world—I think it's there to protect people. I think maybe that's the point.

"What time are we doing pictures?" Terry calls from the kitchen. She came over because *it's about time we got to know each other* and also, *I've got a nice camera*, and also, she and Dad are making and having dinner together tonight.

"I think she'll be here in, like, fifteen." I stand at the kitchen table where Terry is fiddling with her camera (it really is a nice one), changing out a battery pack, and it amazes me how easily she fits in around here. I knew her and Dad were close, but they're so *easy* around each other. It's calming just to be around.

Terry looks up from the batteries and smiles at me. She's got her hair in a long braid again, stray pieces falling out all over the place in charming ways. "You look really nice, Callie."

"Thanks."

There's a knock at the door and I guess it's Mei, but that'd be kind of early, and when I hear my dad open it, he doesn't greet the person loudly like I'd expect. And then I hear a voice I haven't heard in forever.

"Raf?"

And he's there, standing on our porch, talking to Dad all serious and quiet, and when he catches my eye, he doesn't quite smile and neither do I. The cut on his cheek looks a bit less angry than it did before. There are three stitches neatly lined across it.

My dad just kind of steps aside and I follow Rafael outside and wow, it hasn't been that long, but it feels like forever.

"Hey, Catwell."

"Hey, Vega."

He's wearing a suit that fits him surprisingly well. Instead of a pocket square, his bright green bandana is tucked into the front pocket, folded all precisely. "That's nice."

"You look nice."

I smile at him and he smiles at me. I think both of our eyes are kind of watery, and then he's hugging me and I'm hugging him and saying, "What the hell? Where have you been?"

And he's saying, "I'm really sorry."

And I'm saying, "I'm sorry too."

But our apologies aren't really the ones that need to be said.

"I, uh..." he starts. Then he rubs his hands down his face, and he's jumping around on the balls of his feet, and it's all very kinetic. All very much Rafael. "I don't even know what to say... I heard what happened at Martin's. The robbery. I heard you were there."

"Oh." That feels like forever ago. "Yeah. With Mei."

"Yeah. Um. I don't work there anymore."

"I kind of figured."

"I don't... *live* here anymore."

Ah. "So you're living..."

"Um, at the boarding school, in town. Richard's? Everyone's super preppy, it's very weird."

"You like it?"

"It's not so bad."

This is Rafael, but it's Rafael being quiet. Being cautious. It's different. I don't know what to say.

"Why are you all dressed up, then?"

That makes his face light up a bit. He smirks and says, "I've got a date with Jian."

"Really! Really? Wait. Mei told me he wasn't going to prom."

"Oh, we're not. I'm taking him to the movies!"

"You got a tuxedo to go to the movies?"

"Listen, this is a rental. From my roommate." He smiles and I laugh, and then he says, quieter, "And... I gotta impress him, you know?"

"Wasn't he the one that kissed you?"

"Yeah, but..." Rafael runs his hands through his curls a few times. I think he just got a haircut—it's real short on the sides. It looks nice. "You know, I didn't even talk to Jian after that. That night, with Kyle. Like, at all.

"I was supposed to help him with his Spanish class, and just bailed on all the times we had set up. Callie, I didn't talk to anyone from school until three days ago. When I finally called Jian, he straight up called me a dick."

"He did?"

"Yeah. Told me off, yelled at me for like, half an hour."

"Jian yelled at you?"

"Yeah!" Raf kind of laughs at that. But then he's looking at the ground and rubbing at the back of his head. I kind of want to lift his chin up. I don't, but I kind of want to. "This shit with Kyle. Man. This shit fucks with your life. With everyone's life, you know?"

"I'm sorry."

"I'm sorry, too."

Still, it's not us who need to be apologizing, but Kyle isn't going to say sorry. That's what some people do. They wreck you. They rock your life and they'll keep doing it until something makes them stop. And that's it. Then they leave.

Rafael never did anything that warranted the danger he was living in.

But some people don't care about that. Some people will tear and cut and bite at you because they think they're entitled to you and the way you act, the things you do, and the people you love. Some people, when you push them away, will push you right back.

I don't want to give anyone a reason to do the wrong thing. I don't want bad people to be able to prove me right. But I'm figuring it out. I'm learning. I'm thinking maybe some people will hurt you, whether you give them a reason to or not.

I'm thinking no one actually has a reason.

"You were, uh..." I don't know how to go about this. The two of us. It feels like everything is in the open now. Or everything should be. "You were right about Joseph."

"Callie—"

"No, I just mean... he's kind of—" I have to stop. Take

a breath. Then another. "He's awful. And terrible. And... you were right. About that."

"It's not about being right, you know that?" He steps forward and knocks his shoulder into mine. "I don't care if I'm right. I care that you're okay."

"I care that you're okay," I tell him.

"Okay." He smiles. A very small smile.

"Okay." I smile the exact same way. "Will you stay for pictures? I know you're not going to prom, but Mei is gonna be here soon and—"

"Callie. Obviously I'm gonna stay for pictures. I'm always going to stay for pictures."

"My favorite."

"I better be."

"Hey!" Mei squeals and I turn around and see her running towards me in this really flowy, really red dress. Her mom is getting out of the car and waving, and then I really don't see anything because she's hugging me and it's lasting forever.

She smells like strawberries. Or strawberry shampoo. I don't know. It's Mei. And she's warm and I'm smiling. Geez. I can't stop smiling.

We talked about us—Mei and I—and what we mean. We don't want to go through the motions with each other. We want to make sense together. We always did before.

I told her that I don't mind kissing if I'm kissing her. The thought of it otherwise is equally boring and terrifying. We like to hug and be close and touch. And I'm still figuring out how to be in a relationship when you're okay with romance but not the other stuff. I'm figuring it out, and Mei is patient and kind and—I don't know. I guess that this is love and love is easy.

"You look amazing." I say this into her hair, against her shoulder, and she pulls back and looks at me.

"You look incredible."

"Wow. We're both so freaking hot."

Mei nods, very seriously. "Pictures?"

"Pictures."

We stand out in front of the lake because even if we're on the scuzzy end, it's still pretty beautiful out here.

Terry chats with Mei and Mr. and Mrs. Huang while they all take pictures. Dad is smiling and, every now and then, he mutters something to Terry.

Rafael lingers by the side until I wave him towards us.

"You two are my favorite people," I say, just so the three of us can hear.

Mei kisses my cheek and Rafael says something like "Psh," as he wraps an arm around my shoulders.

"Hey," he says. Terry is snapping pictures of us, so Rafael tries to talk through smiling teeth. "Did you ever find that lake monster?"

"Oh yeah." Mei leans in closer to me and I feel like we're all in on something big and crazy and secretive. I don't know; maybe we are.

"Uh, I know it sounds crazy but... yeah. Actually. I saw her again. I know I sound crazy."

Rafael says, "Nah."

And Mei says, "I don't know. Maybe *I* sound crazy, then. Because I definitely believe you." She says it simply, not like she's just playing along with whatever nonsense I'm throwing her way. I guess it does feel a bit crazy to know she's willing to believe in something like a lake monster swimming around in the water behind us.

I squeeze her a little tighter to my side.

I'm driving us to the dance, so Mei's parents hug us both goodbye before heading out. Terry is still taking last-second photos of all of us when Mr. Jones comes outside and offers to take a picture of all of us together. Dad crowds in behind Rafael, Mei, and I, and Terry lingers back for a second before Dad and I wave her in.

And we're all there, together. I think that these are my people. And as we're all huddled next to each other on the cement of the launch point, Lost Lake shimmering behind us, I feel that very strongly. These are the people, the reasons, the legends of my life.

Mr. Jones counts down and the shutter goes off, and I hear something after it. A splash behind us.

When I whip my head around, I see the tail. Her tail. The monster's tail, flicking back into the depths of the lake.

Mr. Jones is staring at the camera and frowning, and I don't want to let myself believe it.

Mr. Jones says, "What the hell?"

And I breathe, "No way."

And everyone else is confused. I think we caught magic on camera.

Because there is lots of magic everywhere, isn't there?

There is a magic to the world that precedes everyone that is in it. It is monsters and fear and nature and love.

It is the stuff that monsters are made of, the stuff that turns planets and shifts skies. You can see it; you can. In dances and smiles and in people who try to hold back tears but can't quite manage to.

I think, if we look at all of the photos we just took, we'd see smiles and friends—good friends—and some kind of peace in our postures and stances. And I think if we look hard enough in that last one, we'll see two rosy pink eyes peeking out from the murky green water of Lost Lake.

I think we'd see magic.

30

A NEW MORNING

THIS MORNING HAS a point and the point is to find a monster.

The two girls are dressed in bulky sweatshirts and are sipping cans of iced tea and paper-cup coffee.

They have already been looking for two hours, even though the sun has only been burning over the lake for one. Their boat is old and green and falling apart just a bit. They paddle through the lake in the same circle they've been paddling all morning and squint into the glassy-green water.

"I swear it was here, just last week. I swear."

"I believe you."

There is a sound, a little splash not far away, and they grab each other's hands because after a nearly silent morning, the sound of something that is not a human voice is a scary, alarming thing.

"Over by the dock!"

The girls quickly paddle over to the noise, each of them taking an oar, as the splash splashes once more.

"There! See! Do you see her!"

"Wow."

There is their monster. Scaly and orange-silver—too slithery to be a fish, too floaty to be a snake. Too big to be anything but unexplainable.

It does not shimmy away from them but instead blinks up from under the wooden slats of the dock. There is a look in its misty pink eyes that makes it seem like maybe, if it could, it would speak and say the most magical things.

The girls look back. Unlike the monster, they *can* speak, but right now, to both of them, speaking feels hard. The monster feels *magic* and they feel *human*.

The monster is patient. The monster has nowhere to be. It looks at their bulky sweatshirts and cans of tea and paper-cup coffee and their falling-apart boat, and it understands the specific mundanities that make a human life fantastic. The monster hypnotizes the girls with the reflection of their own strange magic.

"Hmm," says the friend who has seen this magic before in the monster.

"Hmm," says the friend who has seen this magic before in their life.

Eventually, the sun crawls up a bit higher in the sky and it burns away the fog that lingers on the tops of lakes. The monster decides to move. It ducks under the green boat and jostles the girls, just a bit, as it leaves them.

"Wild. Right?"

"Yes."

"Well, we found the monster, anyway. I just wanted to show you it was there."

"I believed you. Really, I believed you."

ACKNOWLEDGMENTS

Thank you to Emily Oliver and Caitlin Chrismon and everyone at Gen Z who helped to make this story what it is! A big thank you to L. Austen Johnson and All About Book Covers for designing such a lovely cover!

To Jenna Voris and Holly Gary: Thank you so, so much for reading this story and giving notes and talking through weird plot things and just generally being the greatest. You're both incredible writers and incredible people.

Thanks to my family and to Sam and Ellie for being very cool siblings and listening to me explain strange story ideas before they get written or even make sense. I'm glad I'm related to you two.